surviving high school

by Mike Riera

CELESTIAL ARTS

Berkeley • *California*

Celestial Arts Publishing
P.O. Box 7123
Berkeley, CA 94707

Cover design by Libby Oda
Interior text design by Star Type, Berkeley

Printed in the U.S.A.

Library of Congress Cataloging-in-Publication Data

Riera, Michael.
        Surviving high school / Mike Riera.
            p.   cm.
        ISBN 0-89087-825-0
        1. Teenagers–United States–Life skills guides.   2. Adolescence–United States.   3. High school students–United States–Life skills guides.   I. Title.
    HQ796.R5454   1997
    646.7'00835'0973–dc21   96-45273
                                                                CIP

    7 8 9 10 – 07 06 05 04

contents

To Lucia

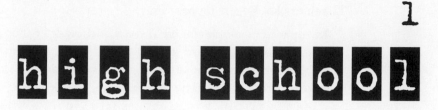

high school

> Good judgment comes from experience,
> and experience comes from bad judgment.
> Mark Twain

Let's be honest, for most of you, high school won't be the best four years of your life. Sure, it's going to have its big moments that will stand out forever, as it should! But on the more day-to-day level, high school means tough decisions and unexpected changes in you and your friends. In fact, you will change as much in these years as in any other four-year period of your life. Hopefully, this book will give you an idea of what to expect, and let you in on what others are thinking and worrying about.

Everyone goes through major upheaval in their personal lives and relationships while in high school, yet unfortunately most high schools are not designed to help you through all these changes. Schools focus 90% of their attention on learning and grades, and 10% on personal development, which is why you need to take charge yourself. And besides, nobody should be making these decisions for you. You need to strengthen your own decision-making muscles, which means lots of trial-and-error learning.

In high school, for the first time, you develop true self-conscious-ness, which at first is completely overwhelming. Nobody escapes this self-consciousness, no matter what it looks like from the outside. Listen to what Roger, 15, has to say:

> At school I work so hard to hold myself together, but inside I'm just a mess. But there's no way I could let this out at school, so I do my best to look like everything is fine. I think everyone does this, but I'm pretty sure I do it more than my friends. Some of them look so relaxed, it just amazes me! I wish I could be more like them.

High school is an emotionally vulnerable time. Though this may feel kind of crazy, it's actually a good thing as emotions are connected to feelings and passions, which are necessary for creativity and excitement. Having strong emotions is healthy – without them you're just a shell of yourself. (Of course, too much of a good thing is still a bad thing.) The bottom line is to listen to your emotions while not letting them bully you around. It's a tough balance to strike, and it takes lots of time, but it's well worth the effort.

The ultimate challenge throughout all these changes is to discover and hold onto your unique spirit – a challenge nobody can do for you. Your spirit is the essential *you* behind all your acts. It's the you that is the same no matter who you're with; the person you answer to late at night when you can't sleep; the you that you find yourself and that no one can take away. You discover your spirit in high school and spend the rest of your life nourishing it and listening to the wisdom it speaks.

Becoming familiar with your true self is no easy task. In fact, it's going to take many courageous acts, some brutal, some ecstatic. Discovering and maintaining your spirit is a "two steps forward, one step backward" experience, starting in high school with one *big* leap forward. We will come back to the concept of discovering your spirit again and again, but for now, take a look at the following table – it summarizes some of the things everybody faces in high school. It doesn't represent any one person's experience exactly; but you can use it as a rough approximation of what to expect. After taking a look at the following table, spend some time thinking about how it affects you. Then try the exercise after it.

	Ninth Grade	**Tenth Grade**	**Eleventh Grade**	**Twelfth Grade**
Physical growth and thinking changes	Girls are slightly ahead of guys; lots of hormones and sexual energy flowing; needing to develop new study habits	Guys are almost caught up; some girls "flirting" with eating disorders and guys "bulking up"; lots of sexual energy	Everyone is more comfortable with themselves; a good sense of your adult body; lots of sexual energy; beginning to think/worry about what comes after high school – work or college?	Most comfortable year, but lots of mixed feelings about graduation and the reality of the future and college/work decisions
Friendship and social development	Want acceptance; working to find a social niche; aware of the party scene	Sorting out friends from acquaintances; grouping around interests like sports, drama, etc; experimenting with the party scene; looking for a girl/boyfriend	Wanting closer friends; getting bored with social scene; changing relationships with adults; driving	Sad to leave friends and concerned about making new ones later; anxious about the future
Family changes	Feel the need for more freedom and independence	Acting on the need for more freedom and independence with your parents, which includes some arguing; talking and confiding in friends more than parents	See parents as people; question their choices; want to be seen as more adult and responsible	Preparing to leave home; changing relationship with parents (whether you leave home or not); excited, sad, and scared *continued* ▶

	Ninth Grade	**Tenth Grade**	**Eleventh Grade**	**Twelfth Grade**
Issues of spirit	Want to fit in and feeling lonely at the same time	Who am I? Why do I act differently with different people? Which is the real me? Need more room from your parents; discovering your passions	Idealistic in many ways; stronger sense of self; contemplating all the shoulds and feeling guilt at unmet expectations	Reflecting and learning; getting more comfortable with who you are

THINK ABOUT IT

This exercise is based loosely on the traditions of several cultures, mainly the Native American culture. The basic idea is to try and by-pass your rational mind in order to gain greater access to your intuitive mind as this is where some of your best and most useful insights will come from. So you want to invite your unconscious mind to share some of its insights with you *now*. For example, everyone is familiar with forgetting someone's name, knowing you know it, but being unable to come up with it despite the fact that it's sitting on the tip of your tongue. You go do something else, get completely into it, and then suddenly the name pops into your head. Your unconscious mind has been working on your behalf while you were otherwise engaged! This exercise is similar; don't try to figure things out in the traditional sense of figuring. Instead, actively invite, and then wait for, the answers to come to you.

You can do the exercise alone or with friends – you decide. It takes ten to fifteen minutes to complete, though you can take as much time as you want.

1. Get four pieces of paper or note cards. Write one of the following questions on each:

    a. What do I want?

    b. Where am I now?

    c. What do I need to do in order to get from where I am to what I want?

    d. What do I need to believe about the world in order to get from where I am to where I want to be?

2. Find a comfortable place (the bigger the better), with room to walk around in, and where you won't be interrupted. (Being outdoors is ideal, but not essential.)

3. Get in a comfortable position, and for 3–5 minutes, simply pay attention to your breathing. Whenever your mind wanders to some idea or thought, gently remind yourself to focus on your breath. (You can either close your eyes or leave them open, whichever feels most comfortable.)

4. Before getting up, pick up the first question and read it to yourself. "What do I want?" Repeat the question over and over to yourself, and then move in whatever direction feels right until your attention naturally comes to rest on something around you – a plant, view, breeze, sound, feeling, or whatever.

5. Stay with whatever has attracted your attention until an answer to your question begins to emerge. You may get a complete answer. Or you might just get the beginnings of an answer in the form of a feeling or image. Pay attention to both subtle and big responses.

6. Do the same with the next three questions, repeating the procedure.

7. Afterward, take some time to write down what happened. Include everything you can – insights, vague feelings and thoughts, etc.

Remember, there are no right or wrong answers – whatever you come up with is right for you. Some of you will get clear responses to all four questions and others will get vague ones, but most of you will fall between the two extremes – you'll get one or two clear insights and the rest will be muddled. If you don't understand what you get, don't worry. It will become clear over time, like it did for Jason, 16:

```
When I did this exercise I didn't understand my
response to the third question. [I had stared
at an oak tree for five minutes.] But now [three
months later] when I'm filling out my college
applications I understand what it's all about.
In fact, as strange as it seems, that's what
my college essay is about — my understanding of
that oak tree.
```

MORE READING:

Changing Bodies, Changing Lives by Ruth Bell and others.

The What's Happening to My Body? Book For Boys by Lynda Madaras with Dane Saavedra.

The What's Happening to My Body? Book For Girls by Lynda Madaras with Area Madaras.

Finding Our Way: The Teen Girls' Survival Guide by Allison Abner and Linda Villarosa.

Ask Me If I Care: Voices From an American High School by Nancy Rubin.

 friendship

Instead of loving your enemies,
treat your friends a little better.
Ed Howe

Friendship and social groups are big things in high school. For some, like Sylvia, 15, they are the focus of high school:

```
Without my friends there's no way I could have
gotten through these last couple of years.
They're the most important people in the world
to me.
```

For people like Russell, 14, friendship is important, but not the only focus:

```
Yeah, my friends are important, but so are other
things. My relationships with my family and
playing baseball are just as important. I try to
keep things pretty much in balance so that if
any one thing gets out-of-sorts it doesn't
throw me for too much of a loop.
```

For still others like Noah, 14, they're a complete source of misery:

I don't have any friends. There are a couple of
guys I talk to at school, but that's it. I never
go anywhere with anybody or talk on the phone.
This is the worst, and nothing I do makes a
difference.

Everybody will probably agree that we all need at least one friend,
since we need the acceptance, support, and companionship they
give. That last part might be the most important – in fact, one psy-
chological theory considers our need to avoid loneliness to be the
strongest organizer of behavior. This is quite a statement in light of
peer pressure.

The meaning and depth of your friendships change as you get
older. As freshmen, most of you would just like to be accepted
by others, especially during lunch when it's really important to
have people to eat with. Some of you, like Florence, 15, prefer to skip
lunch all together rather than face the cafeteria alone, and that's just
fine (believe it or not, you'll end up meeting others like you along
the way):

I don't have any friends at this school yet, so
during lunch I go to the gym and shoot hoops with
a bunch of other people, or go to the computer
room and play games. I just sort of eat my lunch
as I'm walking around. It's not great, but until
I know some people what other choice do I have?

Never fear, by junior year most of this has changed. Sure, acceptance
is still necessary, but a deeper sense of friendship and honesty becomes just as important, as it has for Terry, 17:

I don't need as many friends as I used to, but I
need better friends. I try to really be myself
when I'm with friends, rather than what I think
they want me to be. It's much better this way.

This shift in the way you look at friendship happens to everyone, and
as a result, old groups and circles of friends often change during this
time. That is, people change at different rates and in different direc-
tions. Some people may go through high school with the same friends

8

they've had for ages, but for others, those friendships need to change in terms of depth and diversity. Listen to what happened to Garry, 17, and his group of buddies:

> There were four of us that were always together during freshman and sophomore years. It was like we couldn't do anything unless all of us were together. But now [senior year] it's different. We still do things as a group, only now we do many more things in pairs. And all of us have at least one good friend outside of the original four. Sometimes it's a little strange and tense, but usually things work out fairly well.

Or Sara, 16, and her friends:

> Our group of friends had a big falling out at the end of sophomore year. We were all changing in different ways. Two people wanted the group to stay together forever, and they got resentful of anyone spending time with somebody outside of the group. Finally, we just had this huge blow-up and all went our separate ways. When I look back it seems inevitable, we all had completely different values. I'm surprised we stayed friends as long as we did.

It's also possible to have the best of both worlds. Mara, 16, managed to keep her old friends and meet new ones:

> My friends and I had been together for a few years when I began to feel bored. I wanted to meet some new people with different viewpoints. With my friends it's real safe to do whatever, but that also makes it too predictable. So what I started doing was changing my routines and trying new things, just to see what would happen. I went to a few games, a school dance, a couple of club meetings, and ate lunch by myself in a few different spots. After a few weeks I

had met a couple of new people — well I had known them for a bunch of years, but had just known the most superficial sides of them. We stayed friends all the way through my senior year.

One thing to keep in mind when making new friends is that you have to get past your early judgments of people. We *all* judge people, sometimes positively and sometimes negatively – it's human nature to do so. The trick is to see yourself doing it and then put your judgments aside so you can get a deeper look at the people around you. Having judgments isn't so bad, but not stopping to think about them is. And anyway, people change a lot during high school and probably deserve a second look. If you cling to your judgments you'll probably miss out on some amazing people and things, just like the people who don't look past their judgments of you do! Listen to what happened to Clarissa, 17:

In the summer after junior year I worked at a camp as an assistant counselor. It was the best experience of my life. All the other counselors were older [college students] but they treated me like an equal. Throughout that summer I became much more aware of myself and the world. At the end of camp I couldn't wait for school to start — I wanted to bring this new part of me to my senior year. But it was weird, like nobody could see this new part of me. Everyone kept trying to push me back in the old mold. It was like nobody believed I cared about politics or art — they thought I was just goofing around. It was depressing. The worst part was that I shrank myself back into the mold to fit their judgments of me — I wasn't courageous enough to stand alone.

In part, Clarissa's friends probably weren't really recognizing her changes because they didn't want her to leave their group. The fact that she stayed in the group despite it doesn't mean that Clarissa didn't change and grow, it just means she's changing and growing at a different pace than her friends, which is sometimes hard to accept.

Arguments with Friends

Nobody is perfect (not you or your friends, either!). While friendships are generally relaxing and fun, there are still times when you argue and fight with each other. In fact, unless the arguments are over some moral principle, they're basically par for the course. It may be easy to walk away from people who aren't your friends, but you've got to stick around to work things out with those who are. Frankly, this is never comfortable, but it's usually extremely worthwhile, as Cara, 15, found out with her friend Sasha:

> When Sasha and I had a big fight last semester
> I really doubted whether our friendship would
> make it. But after a bunch of screaming, crying,
> and apologizing we got through it. But that was
> only because we cared for one another so much,
> otherwise it wouldn't have been worth it.

Kianna, 15, takes the situation as a prime opportunity to look at herself:

> Arguing with friends is so annoying, because
> you never win. It's always some sort of compro-
> mise, which is good, because we both get to save
> face. But still, it makes you take a hard look
> at yourself, sometimes harder than you want to
> look.

When you argue with a friend you have to take responsibility for your part in the disagreement, no matter how reluctant you are to do so. Otherwise, the fight will not only destroy your friendship, but will also cause you to miss out on some valuable (OK, even if somewhat *painful*) feedback about yourself. Thomas, 17, has experienced this with one of his friends:

> The fight was really her fault, but still, I kept

it going longer than it had to. It was like some
part of me wanted to punish her. I wanted her to
feel worse than I had felt, which is a terrible
thing to do to a friend.

Arguing is never fun, especially with a friend. The bottom line is not about whether or not you argue, but about what you do after the argument. Working *through* the argument lets you discover a new and better solution and helps you become a better person, like with Fran, 15:

When I realized that our friendship would survive a fight it was just much easier to trust
Sheila and to tell her what I really thought
about things, whether or not she agreed with
me. I felt even more myself with her than
before.

Making friends

Whether it's now while you're in high school, during a summer job or vacation, or during college, you're going to need to know how to make friends. Fortunately, like just about everything else, making friends isn't just about luck, it also involves some basic, *learnable*, skills. Of course, this is not to underestimate the power of being in the right place at the right time and in the right kind of mood. Says Rina, 16:

When Tiffany and I met it was kind of strange.
Most of the time I'm very shy and reserved, but
when we met I was feeling much more outgoing than
normal. I was listening to this great CD in the
store and I was singing to myself — I'm sure
louder than I realized. Then I felt this person looking at me, and when I looked up there
she was. So I just took the headphones off and
said, "It's a great CD. Here, you listen for a
second." After that we just got into this great
conversation, and we have been best friends
ever since.

While you can't make luck happen, you can give it some help. Start by changing your routines or trying different things, since it moves you away from familiar places and faces. How is someone new supposed to discover *you* if you stay stuck in the same routine? You have nothing to lose – even if you don't meet your next best friend, you get some practice talking with people you don't know, and will probably learn some new things about yourself, too. So, shake things up and invite some luck into your life (but be sure to remember to detach yourself from your judgments of others and yourself before you do). This friend of mine who's a writer has this to offer:

```
Whenever I get stuck I will go for the same
walk everyday. But each day I pretend that I'm
somebody else, so I see the things around me
differently each day. One day I pretend I'm a
painter and try to look around me as I imagine
a painter would. The next day I might pretend
to be a contractor; the next, an electrician;
the next, an environmentalist; the next, a
homeless person; the next, a developer with
lots of money; and the next, a dancer. After
a few days of this my senses wake up and I see
all sorts of new perspectives.
```

Let's assume you get the luck thing working in your favor (believe me, it will happen) – what you need now are a few skills. You have more control over friendship skills, and you can practice them whenever you want. While these skills ultimately involve big qualities like trust, loyalty, honesty, fairness, and compassion, they also include more mundane things like making conversation and developing a sense of humor. Becoming a good conversationalist is actually much easier than it seems, especially when you realize one key point – *most people enjoy talking about themselves*. In other words, what's absolutely most important for good conversation is good listening (and you don't have to be outgoing to be adept at that!). When you really listen to what people say, your curiosity inevitably gets the better of you, and without even realizing it you'll find yourself with lots of interesting questions to ask and points to make. Jaclyn, 16, agrees:

Whenever people meet me they think I'm such a
good conversationalist, but they don't realize
how shy I am and how hard I had to work to get
comfortable talking to people. I learned a lot
by listening to radio interviews and trying
to figure out how the interviewer came up with
their next point or question. It all boiled down
to good listening and staying interested. So
that's what I do, and it usually makes for easy
conversation.

Listening and curiosity go together. The more you practice the better you get. All of us have more friendship-making skills and experiences than we realize, so before finishing, try this:

THINK ABOUT IT

1. Think of two friends you have had at different times in your life. Maybe one is a current classmate and the other is someone you met at camp during the third grade.

2. Think back on how you met each other, and more importantly, how you became friends. When did you first realize you were friends? What happened to bring you from being acquaintances to becoming friends?

3. From each of your friend's perspective, what makes (or made) you a good friend?

MORE READING:

Social Savvy: A Handbook for Teens Who Want to Know What to Say, What to Do, and How to Feel Confident in any Situation by Judith Re with Meg F. Schneider.

3

romance

> Whoever named it necking was a
> poor judge of anatomy.
>   Groucho Marx

By high school, most people are at least thinking about the possibility of romance (if you're not, that's OK, there's plenty of time). Given all the changes you're going through, a girlfriend or boyfriend makes a lot of sense because a good relationship makes everything else easier. A boyfriend or girlfriend can give you security, acceptance, and love. The relationship can also act as a great buffer between you and the rest of the world, as Amanda, 17, has found:

> Since I started seeing Raceed [seven months
> earlier] my life has been much better. It isn't
> that I'm living through him either — it's that
> he helps me feel more secure about myself. I
> feel stronger as a person. All my old problems
> are still there, but now they don't seem as bad
> as they used to.

And Jason, 16:

> Kathy and I have been together for about five

16

months now, but it seems like longer. We are
already best friends. Even though it isn't,
life seems much simpler with her around. We
trust each other enough to be honest with one
another, which really helps. Honestly, sometimes
you don't know who you can trust, so having
somebody you can always count on is a big help.

While serious romance in high school is not unheard of, short-lived
romances (and particularly crushes) are way more common. All romance offers some degree of security, trust, and friendship – the degree just depends on the intensity of the relationship. In the *ideal*
romance you get to explore intimate feelings and sexual behaviors
with somebody you respect, care for, and trust. You can be more
yourself with this person than with anybody else. There's also another
added bonus – you get to discover parts of yourself you didn't even
know existed, like Sean, 15, did:

Since Cara is really into drama I decided to
give it a try myself. I didn't think it was for
me, but I was wrong. The drama teacher said I
have a natural stage voice. Now I have a small
part in the next school production.

What can be a problem is having preconceived notions about what,
exactly, the perfect relationship is. It's a rare thing to have fantasies
about the perfect relationship match the real world experience of
one. Once the blissful part of having actually found someone wears
off, real issues raise their heads and you have to decide how important the relationship is to you. One common fantasy is the one where
you think that if you just had a girl/boyfriend, your life would go
from awful to wonderful, like Bill, 17, had:

For two years I dreamed about having a steady
girlfriend, someone who I could be closer to
than anyone else in my life – a best friend *and*
a lover. Then, when Sandra came along it was
like my dreams were answered. I was as happy
as I had ever been in my life during those first

couple of months. But then I realized that while
having a girlfriend solved a lot of my problems —
loneliness in particular — it brought along
other problems like not always being able to do
what I wanted to do when I wanted to. I had to
consider what she wanted. We had to make plans,
whereas I had always done things spontaneously.
Sometimes, when we argued it was like we were
parent and kid. This is what finally did us in,
neither one of us was ready to be tied down
like that.

A second common fantasy is the one where you think there is a perfect man or woman for you. Says Sylvia, 15:

Every time I go out with somebody it follows the
same pattern. I get a crush on the guy; we go
out; we fall madly in love; I start to see problems with him that I never noticed before; we
start to argue a lot; and we break-up, vowing
not to talk to each other again. It takes about
two weeks.

A third fantasy, as shown by Terrel, 18, is where you think that a boy/girlfriend would make your already good life perfect:

I wasn't even really looking for a girlfriend,
but when Christy came along it was too perfect
to pass up. It was especially good because she
got along with my friends and family, which
I had been worried about. But after awhile I
felt all this pressure from people. I felt my
friends leaving me out of things and forgetting
to include me in their plans because they just
figured I would be with Christy. Then my parents
started getting on me about being too serious
with her. And after the initial infatuation
faded I realized we didn't have a lot in common,
we were both just real horny. But having just
that wasn't worth it to either of us.

People outside the relationship

When you first start going out with someone, your friends are probably going to be real supportive, and your parents are going to at least be neutral. Then a strange thing often happens – as you get happier and more committed to this person, your friends and family get less supportive. Aaron, 15, describes this experience:

> Everyone was psyched when Karen and I got
> together. All our friends thought we were per-
> fect for each other. But after awhile my friends
> started rolling their eyes or giving each other
> looks when I mentioned her name. Then they
> started to give me grief whenever I made plans
> with her. It was like they were jealous of her.

What you've got to realize in this situation is that time spent with your girlfriend or boyfriend is time *not* spent with your friends. Your friends, like Donna's, 16, feel this as rejection:

> I'm really confused. Stephen and I have a great
> relationship, but I've had my friends for the
> past six years. Suddenly I feel like I have to
> choose between them. He wants more of my time
> and so do my friends. No matter what I decide
> to do someone is disappointed.

The fact of the matter is that you probably already had a full life before you even started seeing this person, so what you have to do now is a little reorganization. The ultimate goal is to strike a balance between the important activities and people in your life, and your new romance. Sophie, 16, learned the hard way:

> I really blew it. When I started seeing Jeff
> I just focused on him. I totally neglected my
> friends. At first they were hurt, but pretty soon
> after they just got pissed and blew me off.
> It bothered me at the time, but I just couldn't
> understand how they could be so selfish and not
> understanding of me. Then when Jeff and I broke
> up I had nobody to turn to. I was all alone at

one of the worst times in my life. My friends had warned me of this but I hadn't been paying attention. It was a terrible year.

Like it or not, when you start seeing somebody regularly it is *your* responsibility to make sure you keep spending time with your friends, too. They need to feel that they're still important to you, and it's best to show this by what you do, rather than what you say. When you make a point to spend time with your friends, you make it easier for them to support you in this relationship. Again (and you're going to get sick of hearing this), this is not an easy task, and you have to get ready to take a few rejections along the way, but it'll be worth the effort. Leslie, 16, knows this well:

I really worked to make sure my friends knew how important they were to me when I started seeing Zach. I made sure to call them and make plans with them. I've seen too many classmates forget about their friends when they started seeing somebody. And it wasn't easy. Lots of times they said no to my plans or called me at the last minute to do something when they already knew I had plans with Zach. I felt like that was their way of making me feel what it was like to be rejected, so I always tried to keep to myself about it.

Stephen, 16, experienced something similar:

I was lucky, when I started seeing Emily a couple of my friends got girlfriends too. All of us decided that Fridays were our nights to do things together, and we stuck to it. Since then all of us have broken up with or been broken up with by those girls, but we're still friends and still together every Friday night.

Breaking up

Though it's tough to admit it, we can probably all agree that most high school relationships are going to end in a break up. There are certainly exceptions, but for the most part you will not spend the rest of your life with your first boyfriend or girlfriend. And while this may hurt to hear, it's also good in the long run. (Understand that this isn't meant to underestimate the intensity or love you may feel – that's very real.) Having these relationships is how you get romantic relationship experience, all of which will come in real handy when you do finally meet the right person. So don't be afraid of a little hurt now; it will make you a better partner later on, when there's even more at stake.

Suffice it to say that if you have ventured into the world of romance, you will most likely experience a break up. Whether you do the breaking up or are the one broken up with, the experience is still painful, sad, and confusing, as Mike, 15, found:

> It was so weird. Our relationship was fading fast and I was getting ready to break up with her myself, but she beat me to it. But instead of being relieved I was angry, and then real sad. At first I tried to romance her back, but that didn't work at all. Then I got nasty — I called her all sorts of names, left terrible messages on her answering machine, and gave her the dirtiest looks in the world. Through all this I really wanted to go back out with her. The sick part is that I think I wanted to go back out with her just so I could break up with her!

Or Rachel, 18:

> We'd been going out for a long time and besides being girlfriend and boyfriend we were best friends. From early on we swore to one another that if we ever broke up we would stay close friends. We both believed this. Then, after one year of going out we finally split up — he broke up with me. At first we were real nice to one another. We talked like rational people, we even still did things together. But the whole time it felt fake to me. Then one day it just

exploded — we had both been pretending everything was fine when it wasn't. We ended up really hating one another for a long time after that. Finally, at graduation, we talked. We both want to be friends in the future, but we'll just have to wait and see.

Or Jessie, 16:

I think it is definitely harder to be the one on the receiving end of the break up — you feel totally rejected. It sucks. You are completely powerless. All you want to do is scream or punch somebody.

Or Connie, 16:

It's much harder if you are the one that starts the break up because you feel so guilty. It's terrible having to tell somebody you don't want to see them anymore — to have to see that hurt look cross their face is awful. Then of course you know the anger is coming right after that. In fact, whenever I want to break up with somebody I usually start acting like a jerk, hoping that they'll break up with me instead. I know it's kind of wimpy, but still, it's better than being the bad guy.

Clearly, there are a million different responses out there, and there's simply no right way to break up, or to be broken up with. There are, however, some things to remember.

If you are the one breaking up:

- Be direct. Don't wait for them to pick up on your hints, it only hurts more.
- Don't try to overanalyze your decision. Relationships are not rational, so don't try to make the break up rational, even if the other person insists on knowing "why." Trust your feelings.

- Be honest. Don't say something to be nice unless you believe it. There's no way to soften the blow, and trying to do so only insults the other person. At the same time, don't be needlessly harsh; the other person is very vulnerable now, whether they look it or not.

If you are the one being broken up with:
- Don't argue with their reasons. You can't talk them out of it, and if you can, then it won't last.
- Tell them how it feels, even if it hurts them. Take care of yourself, not them.
- Get away from them for awhile to collect your thoughts and feelings. Spend some time with friends.

Of course, once you have broken up you may get back together again. In fact, if the relationship was long and serious, you probably *will* have a bunch of mini-relationships, or flings, with that same person for a small stretch of time. While this is confusing, it's not unusual. Even if you were absolutely certain and initiated the break up, going from being a twosome to being by yourself again can be a drag, as Karen, 15, found out:

```
When I broke up with Jessie I was very sure of
myself, but a week later I was having my doubts.
I was having a hard time remembering why I had
been so sure of myself. Suddenly all I could
remember were the good parts of the relation-
ship. I was lonely, and none of my friends could
understand. So it wasn't all that surprising,
at least to me, when we got together a couple of
weeks later at a party. We even started going
out again for a while. But very quickly I remem-
bered why I had wanted to break up in the first
place. That was three months ago, and we have
gotten together since then from time to time,
but it never works out. I think we're just
weaning ourselves from one another.
```

And Belinda, 16:

> It's so strange, one day he's telling me he
> doesn't want to see me anymore and a week later
> we're all over each other in the backseat of his
> car! At first, whenever this happened I was hop-
> ing that we would get back together, but after a
> while I realized it just wasn't going to happen.
> And each time it happens the scene afterwards
> gets uglier and uglier. He broke up, but I have
> to say no. It isn't fair.

So if you find yourself having these relapses, go easy on yourself. Yeah, it's confusing, and yeah, it hurts, but it's also a sign of how much you cared for one another. Believe it or not, this same thing happens with lots of adults after they get separated or divorced – some of them even remarry.

THINK ABOUT IT

Which do you think is more difficult, to break up with someone or to be broken up with? Why?

4

sex

We all worry about the population explosion,
but we don't worry about it at the right time.
Arthur Hoppe

Ideally, sex and romance go together. What that really means is that sex *without* romance is generally a bad idea; sex *in order to achieve romance* is an even worse one. On the other hand, romance with sex can be wonderful, but so can romance without sex. What I'm saying here is that romance by itself is more powerful and fulfilling than just plain sex. Devon, 16, seems to agree:

> Me and my girlfriend have been together over
> a year and we really love one another. We do
> pretty much everything physically with one
> another except intercourse. Being in love and
> being loved is the best part of our relation-
> ship, so we're going to wait for the sex part
> until we're both ready.

So does Cecilia, 17:

> I can't even imagine having sex without loving
> the person I'm with. Making love is such a

vulnerable and intimate thing to do. An important part of the experience is wanting to and
being able to cuddle with one another afterwards. If I didn't love the person I was with
it would be awful. I would just be trying to get
out of there as soon as possible, all the time
wondering what I got myself into.

Or Charles, 17:

When you're with somebody you care about,
it [making love] is such a tender experience.
It brings you even closer together. But if it
is just for the sex it brings you too close
together, so you have no choice but to get away
as soon as possible. And one of the people
always gets hurt, no matter what anybody says.

And Lila, 16:

Once I tried to get this guy to fall for me by
having sex with him. I teased him for awhile but
finally "gave in." It didn't work. It was horrible. Not only did he not fall for me, but he
told all his friends about me and pretty soon
all these guys were hitting on me — expecting
that I would have sex with them!

Dealing with your sexual energy is a part of growing up. Make no
mistake about it, this energy is strong, and seems overbearing at
times. As Milton, 15, point out, it's hard to escape it:

I mean even when I try to get sex off my mind
it's impossible. It's everywhere — in magazines,
on television, and even on billboards! I can't
get away from it no matter which way I turn.

This energy is real — don't worry, you're not the only person feeling
it. Look around at your classmates, they're all feeling it too (although
maybe no one's talking about it). For some of you, masturbation

might be an outlet for this energy, but not everyone is comfortable with that. Obviously, it's a personal decision. Just know that all of your classmates are wrestling with their sexual energy, too.

Now to the big question: "When will I be ready for sex?" First off, be clear about the fact that only you know the answer. Still, gathering opinions and information and listening to how other people have answered this question will all help you clarify your thoughts. After all, your first time only happens once. Gretchen, 17, says:

> For me, I had to feel like the other person was willing to wait as long as I wanted. Whenever I felt pressured at all it was a sign that I should wait longer. It took awhile, but finally one day I just knew I was with the right person and I was ready. It was scary at first, but it turned out great. I have no regrets having had sex or for waiting so long.

Or Lynda, 15:

> I had planned it out in my head for years. My first experience with sex was supposed to be with someone I loved and cared for deeply. Instead I got drunk one night and had sex with one of my friends. Not only was it awful, but it also ruined our friendship. We don't know how to treat one another anymore.

Alcohol and hormones are as dangerous together as alcohol and cars are, leading to more regrets than most are willing to admit. When people get drunk, good decision making goes out the window, leaving everyone vulnerable to bad decisions. Says Dana, 15:

> After helping my friend through her first sexual experience — basically date rape after her date got her really drunk — I have only one rule. When I have sex for the first time I will make sure that I am completely sober.

When you *do* make the decision to have sex, be sure to educate yourself about it first (if you haven't already). Specifically, get some information about birth control methods and ways to reduce your risk for sexually transmitted diseases. It's difficult to enjoy sex if you're concerned about pregnancy or disease – if nothing else, it leaves you worried afterwards. There's really no excuse – this kind of information is available in most schools, or from your local Planned Parenthood (check the phone book for listings). Reggie, 16, talks about how he prepared:

> When I was thinking about having sex for the first time I went to see the health teacher at school. I wanted to talk, but I also wanted to get some condoms [his school gives out condoms to students that request them]. She was pretty cool to talk to. I took the condoms, but decided to wait on the sex.

And be sure to follow through with using the methods you've chosen. It's difficult because, as you probably realize, what you *know* about sex, pregnancy, and disease from your classroom or counselor is very different from what you'll *remember* on a hot, Saturday-night date. Listen to Amber, 16:

> I'm the one that goes to middle schools to talk to kids about sex and birth control. Maybe I should listen to myself someday. Last weekend Jason and I really got into it, and before I knew it we were having unprotected sex. Now I'm just praying for my period.

Given the horror of a disease like AIDS it's also a good idea to talk to your partner about their health, even though it might seem like an awkward conversation. Says David, 16:

> I knew Beth had had a couple of serious boy-friends before me and that she had sex with both of them. But this was the first time for me. So before anything happened I asked her if she had ever taken an AIDS test. She got really freaked

28

out. But I figure if we can't talk about this
then we're not ready for sex.

And Lydia, 17:

Sam got real mad when I asked him if he had ever
been tested for AIDS. He thought I was calling
him a slut or something. But after awhile he
understood that it wasn't about that at all. We
ended up having a good conversation, and then
we both went in and got tested together. That
was real scary — not the test, but waiting for
the results.

A good rule of thumb is that if you can't talk about these things with
your partner, then you should wait to have sex. Or as a retired health
teacher used to tell her students:

If you have any doubts, wait. I know it seems
like forever, but at sixteen you have at least
fifty years of good sex ahead of you, if you make
sure you don't jump without looking. Look at me,
I'm sixty and still going strong!

Forced sex

Sadly, rape and date rape are realities that everyone needs to acknowledge. (If you have been raped, you should definitely speak with
a professional counselor who can help you.) While rape is pretty easy
to define, date rape is frequently more vague and is often not recognized until weeks after the event, as it was for Sophie, 14:

I had said no a bunch of times, but because he
kept insisting I finally just kept quiet and went
along. But it wasn't until yesterday when I was
reading an article about date rape that I had
a name for what happened to me. It was awful,
and the worst part was that I felt it was my
fault.

Ideally, saying *no* is understood as *no*, but *no* seems to mean different things to different people. What is most important is that *you know what* no *means to you*, and that you stick to it (there is more about this in the chapter on Personal Safety, beginning on page 117). Jenni, 16, talks about how confusing it can be:

> He was all over me. I mean it was kind of nice, but it was just too fast. I kept telling him to slow down, and he would — for about a second. Finally I just said to stop, but within a few minutes he was back at it again. I ended up having to yell at him to stop. He got that I was serious when he saw me start to get up and leave. Then it was cool — he was sorry and didn't try anything like that again. But wow, it was confusing there for a few minutes.

Or Gayle, 15:

> No matter what I said he just kept on going. When I told him I would scream if he kept at it he just laughed and kept going. Then when I screamed he flipped out. But I had to show him that I was serious.

Remember, it's your body, so you need to be comfortable with the pace and intensity of what's happening to it. If you need to pause and collect your thoughts, then you should, and you never have to apologize for slowing things down. Sometimes, the other person is relieved, too, like Eduardo, 16, was:

> I know it sounds strange, but I was glad when she told me to slow down. (I was getting a little crazed.) It was important to me that she enjoy it as much as I did, and if slowing down was what she needed then that was fine with me. I mean I'm not an animal that can't stop himself.

THINK ABOUT IT

While only you can know when you're ready for sex, these questions should help you get clear on a few things before reaching any conclusions.

1. Do *you* think there's any difference between sexual intercourse and making love? If so, what is it?

2. How do you imagine you will feel about it the next day if you have sex? If you don't?

3. Have you *both* thought about and discussed different means of birth control? If not, what's stopping you?

4. Does making love have the same meaning for you as it does for your partner?

MORE READING:

Finding Your Way: A Book About Sexual Ethics by Susan Neiburg Terkel.

Boys And Sex by Wardell Pomeroy.

Speaking Out: Teenagers Talk on Race, Sex, and Identity by Susan Kukin.

5

#

If you removed all of the homosexuals and
homosexual influence from what is generally
regarded as American culture, you would be
pretty much left with "Let's Make A Deal."
Fran Leibowitz

Between five and ten percent of high school students are gay. If you
are one of these five to ten percent, then this, more than any other
single fact, dominates your life right now. Stan, 16, talks about his
experience:

> Once I realized I was gay nothing else seemed
> important. At first I was terrified that people
> would somehow figure it out. It was like I was
> afraid people could read my mind. Then, in
> everything I did, I tried to make sure I acted
> like a straight person, whatever that meant.
> I was really afraid that if people found out
> they would make fun of me and ditch me as a
> friend. I thought about it constantly.

What is really sad is that many of Stan's fears are real. Many people are still not very accepting of homosexuality, and so many gays feel like they should be cautious in expressing their sexuality, and for good reasons. Jeremy, 18, says:

> I realized I was gay in middle school, but I
> still haven't come out to any of my friends
> [four years later as a senior]. We insult each
> other by calling one another "faggot," so how
> could I ever expect them to accept me? I'm just
> going to make sure I go far away to college and
> never move back to this town.

People have no choice with their sexuality – same with their race or gender. It just doesn't work that way. And, it can be quite a blow to the person involved, as shown by Charlene, 17:

> I mean at first I pretended I wasn't having these
> kinds of feelings about other girls, but that
> didn't last too long. Then I figured I could
> pretend — that actually lasted awhile. I even
> had a steady boyfriend for most of junior year.
> But finally I realized I couldn't pretend and
> I couldn't change, I had to deal with it. Of
> course this all sounds pretty neat and easy, but
> it was far from it. I attempted suicide a couple
> of times before I ever started to deal with being
> gay, it was so scary.

Experts say that gay teenagers have a significantly greater risk of suicide than non-gay students do because of the isolation and fear they usually experience. Many gay teenagers (and even adults) fear that their family and friends will reject them if they find out. Many of us have a hard time imagining something about ourselves that is so difficult to accept that suicide becomes a real option, but this is the sad truth for many gay teenagers. The fear of rejection can be so strong that suicide seems the only way out, as it did to Terrel, 16:

> Realizing I was gay was about the worst moment
> of my life. I could have handled anything better
> than being gay. I just freaked out for a few

```
months there. I ran away, lived on the streets,
shot up, and even whored myself. Then one day it
got so bad I put a gun to my head. I was just
starting to pull the trigger when this little
voice in my head went off and told me to put the
gun down and to show some courage. That was nine
months ago, and there is no way I would try to
kill myself today.
```

If you are gay

Once you realize you are gay, you have a couple of tough decisions ahead of you: 1. Do you tell anybody (come out)? If so, who? And, 2. Are you going to be sexually active? If so, with whom and where?

Before coming out to anybody you need to make sure you're ready and able to deal with the possibility of them either denying what you're saying or maybe even rejecting you as a person. It's best to prepare for the worst so you're not caught off guard. Even if your friends and parents talk about their acceptance of homosexuality, it's still going to surprise and maybe even shock them to learn that you are gay. Says Denise, 16:

```
My parents are these wild-eyed liberals, so I
figured they would understand. I didn't think
it would even be a big deal to them. When I told
them my mom started crying and my dad started
walking around like a caged tiger. He even asked
me if I was sure! Then mom suggested it might
just be a phase! It got ugly real quick. I ended
up spending a few nights away from home before
we slowly started to sort through it all.
```

There are organizations out there that can help both you and your parents deal with this. The best known organization is P-FLAG – Parents and Friends of Lesbians and Gays (P.O. Box 20308, Denver, CO, 80220). By all means give this address to your parents. P-FLAG offers parents support and guidance while they learn to accept and love a gay child. Many, many parent-child relationships have been saved by this organization, as Joel, 16, attests:

My parents were so out of it when I came out to
them, and I wasn't much help. I didn't have any
patience with them. But after they got in touch
with other parents — through P-FLAG — I could see
that they were really trying to understand, it
was just going to take awhile. But that made
sense, it took me awhile to come to grips with
being gay, so I guess I couldn't expect them to
do it in one day.

It's also a good idea for *you* to talk to others who have already come out
before you tell anyone. Look in the phone book for a Gay and Lesbian
Hot Line to call, or for local support groups of Gay and Lesbian Youth
to attend. It helped Charlotte, 15, to cope with her own feelings:

The first time I went to a support group for gay
and lesbian teenagers I was pretty doubtful. I
mean all I knew about them was that they were
gay. And what if I didn't like them! It turned
out that being a gay teenager was enough to have
in common. It just felt so liberating to be able
to say aloud all the conversations I had been so
careful to keep to myself. Hearing that others
have the same thoughts and feelings was real
helpful, too.

These groups let you see how others dealt with the issue of coming
out and give you support in doing it yourself. These are also great
places to talk about what it's really like to be a gay teenager, which as
Chris, 16, points out, is not an easy thing:

When I was getting ready to come out to my parents a couple of older guys in the group were
real helpful. They helped me think through the
possible reactions my parents could have along
with helping me to make sure I was ready to come
out to them. Then afterwards they called regularly to see how things were going.

And Stephanie, 16:

After my first visit to the support group I was
determined to come out to my friends at school,
but a couple of the girls in the group ques-
tioned me about that. They wondered if I wasn't
letting my enthusiasm get the best of me. It was
enough to make me stop and think. I decided not
to tell them — the risks were too much, and at
this point, no matter how superficial, I couldn't
afford to be without friends at school.

Even if you're the kind of person who doesn't like groups, particularly support groups, it's a good idea to try it out at least once. As
Brooke, 17, points out, it may still boost your confidence:

I read about the group in the paper one day and
spontaneously went. This is not like me — I hate
the idea of support groups. It was pretty weird,
but it did help me see that I'm not alone. It
also helped me realize that I could do it without a support group, so I haven't gone back, and
don't plan to either.

Finally, if you do come out, remember what Joel said earlier. It takes
time to recognize and accept homosexuality in yourself, so it will
take your friends and family some time, too. Be patient with them –
it's well worth it!

THINK ABOUT IT

Imagine that the way you feel towards the opposite sex is considered
wrong by much of society. Imagine that the social norm – on television and in magazines – is for people of the same sex to be romantic
with one another. Furthermore, imagine hearing your family and
friends making jokes about "those damn heterosexuals."

1. How does it feel to be one of these damn heterosexuals? Does it
   make you nervous? Ashamed? Embarrassed? Scared?

2. Would you come out to your parents? Family? Friends? Why or why not?

3. Would you date other heterosexuals in high school? If so, how open would you be about it? Would you take a heterosexual date to the prom?

Also, if you learned that a friend was gay, what could you do or say to support him or her? If you're gay, what can friends do to support you?

MORE READING:

Free Your Mind: The Book For Gay, Lesbian, and Bisexual Youth by Ellen Bass and Kate Kaufman.

Lesbians and Gays and Sports by Deane Perry Young.

On Being Gay: Thoughts on Family, Faith, and Love by Brian McNaught.

Two Teenagers In Twenty: Writings by Gay and Lesbian Youth by Ann Heron (Editor).

6

getting your driver's license

The best way to keep children home is to
make the home atmosphere pleasant —
and let the air out of the tires.
Dorothy Parker

Most of you are going to want to start driving when you turn sixteen,
which means you are going to need to get a driver's license. Others of
you, like Kim, 16, are just not interested in the license, don't feel ready,
or don't want the responsibility of it or the hassle with your parents:

> I live in a city with a decent transportation
> system, so there is no real need for me to drive.
> I just don't want the bother right now, maybe
> when I go to college — depending on where that is.

But if you're like Seth, 15 (and most of you probably are), getting
your driver's license is something you've looked forward to for a long
time:

> I have been thinking and planning to get my
> license since I was fourteen. I already have
> money saved to pay for insurance and driver's
> school, and I have even begun preparing for the
> written test. I'm psyched!

Without a doubt, getting your driver's license – and, even more importantly, access to a car – dramatically changes your life. Driving gives you more freedom and independence, and in fact, for many like Gregor, 16, the car becomes your home away from home:

```
My friends and I love to just drive around on a
weekend night. We're always looking to hook up
with other friends, but it really doesn't mat-
ter if we find anybody else. In the car we can
do whatever we want — say whatever comes to mind
without having to worry about a parent eaves-
dropping, play whatever music we want and as
loud as we want, and go wherever we like, maybe
a friend's house, a food place, or whatever.
```

Parents: Getting and keeping your license

An important part of getting and keeping your driver's license is to make sure that your parents feel like good parents along the way. They need to feel that they're making a good decision by letting you drive, and if they feel any hint of irresponsibility, they will block the path to your license. Listen to what Christopher, 44, said about his son, Steve:

```
It felt like Steve was trying to pull one over
on us. We didn't feel good about his getting his
license — we were actually feeling like bad par-
ents — and Steve didn't do anything to help. He
just kept insisting that he deserved it. And
sure, what he had to say made sense, but somehow
it didn't feel right at all. As a result, we
kept coming up with unconscious obstacles like
forgetting to call the insurance agent, "losing"
his permit after he gave it to us to sign, or
not having the time to take him driving. It was
miserable for all of us.
```

When getting your license, it helps to understand your parents' perspective. Essentially, they want you to learn to drive, as it's a sign of the good job they've done and of the responsible adult you're becoming. Your job is to emphasize the "responsible, young adult" side of your nature, and so minimize their concerns. Say Gita, 42:

```
I know it sounds arch-conservative and all, and I
can't believe I'm going to say what I'm going to
say, but I'm too afraid for my daughter's safety
to let her drive. Now don't get me wrong, I trust
her completely, it's the other drivers on the
road that I don't trust. So right now, I'm almost
willing to have her hate me for not letting her
drive so that I can be sure she'll be around to
have a relationship with in five years.
```

Sounds crazy, but remember, many parents associate your driving with inevitable disaster – whether you're the responsible party or not. Unfortunately, the media doesn't do much to discourage this thinking. I guarantee you have never seen the following article in your local paper:

"FOUR TEENS DRIVE TO PARTY, HAVE GREAT TIME, AND GET HOME SAFELY!"

On Saturday evening four seventeen-year-old high school students drove to and attended a local party. They were under the impression that because the host's parents were home no alcohol was being served. They had assured their parents that this was the case in order to get permission to attend and to use the car. But when they arrived, to their shock, the parents were upstairs while the party was raging below. Apparently the parents had bought their daughter a keg for the party! Rather than leave, the four teens stayed for the party. Two of them drank some beer and two did not (the driver did not drink). Over the course of the night they witnessed the predictable pattern of kids drinking too much, insulting one another, and eventually getting sick, but most everybody else just hung out and talked — periodically laughing at or worrying about their drunk friends. They were having a good time so they waited until the last minute to go home — two of the teens had a curfew of 12:30 am. After just making the curfew, the other two teens stopped at a local all-night diner for some food. Both arrived home safely at around 1:15.

Mostly you and your parents see headlines like "Teens' Car Struck By Drunk Driver, One Dies and Two in Critical Conditon," so part of your job is to show your parents the positive stories they don't get through the media. See how Shelby, 15, does it:

> I'm always telling my parents about how respon-
> sible my friends are that drive. You know, things
> about the designated driver and the good-student
> discount for car insurance. I also always have
> my friends come in when they pick me up, so my
> parents can see how many of my friends already
> drive.

It's also important that you all sit down and openly discuss the disasters that *do* happen. Your ability to recognize and discuss these issues shows your parents that you're aware of the dangers and relieves much of their worry. If you just dismiss it all with a wave of your hand, your parents will worry even more. Note how Karen's actions allayed her father's fears:

> After the bad crash at school last year [one
> student was killed and two were seriously in-
> jured when their car ran off a country road late
> at night] Karen didn't wait for us to bring it
> up. She brought the subject up to us directly,
> including her ideas of what could have gone
> wrong (including the use of alcohol) and how the
> disaster might have been avoided. It was a tense
> conversation for all of us, especially consid-
> ering that Karen is due to take her driver's
> test next month, but in the end I was strangely
> relieved. Her willingness to discuss this com-
> plex issue without getting defensive allowed me
> to see how responsible she is — probably respon-
> sible enough to drive a car. That conversation
> really turned a corner for me, because now I
> feel like a good parent by allowing her to drive,
> rather than a bad parent giving in to peer and
> societal pressure that has magically declared
> the age of 16 as mature enough to drive a car.

Take the time to be open with your parents about what it means for you to get your driver's license — the expense (discussed in the Money chapter, beginning on page 139), the responsibility, *and* the dangers. Your awareness will inspire their support, and make them more comfortable with the whole idea – something both of you will benefit from!

THINK ABOUT IT

1. If you don't yet have your license, what do you need to do to get it? (List things like arranging for the exam, getting access to a car, and getting insurance.)

2. What do you need to show or tell your parents so that they can feel good about you driving?

3. If you already have your license, how can you remind your parents of your responsible, aware nature so that they *continue* to feel good about you driving?

alcohol and drugs

The chains of habit are too weak to be
felt until they are too strong to be broken.
Samuel Johnson

Alcohol and drugs are the stuff that really terrifies parents, making it difficult for you to talk to them about it. Unfortunately, as it was with driving, the media only scares them more. By high school, the issue of using or not using either alcohol *or* drugs is more a question of desire than availability. That is, the decision to use at all, what to use, or how much to use, rests squarely in your hands. Shelly, 17, agrees:

```
Yeah, I can pretty much get whatever booze I
want without much trouble. There are lots of
people with fake IDs who buy for me and stores
that sell directly to me. I even have my own
fake ID, I just haven't had the courage to use
it yet. They [fake IDs] are pretty easy to get,
too. Lots of people make them at school — it
costs about $20 to get a decent one.
```

Since the main purpose of this book is to help you decide on what, if any, relationship you're going to have with drugs and alcohol, I'm not going to discuss either the types available or their effects. In general, however, if you decide to use something, it's a good idea to learn more about what you're using and how it works in your body. There are many good books that do this, one of which is listed at the end of this chapter.

Why use?

There are many reasons why people use drugs and alcohol. One common reason is that these substances reduce your inhibitions and self-consciousness, making you more spontaneous and fun. They tend to make you feel closer to people and more confident, although depending on your mood, the opposite can also be true. There is nothing inherently wrong with these reasons for using, so long as you don't rely on drugs or alcohol for your social life. Everyone has to learn spontaneity and self-confidence without alcohol or drugs, as Luke, 17, has learned:

> At first I just drank because my friends were really into it. But then I came to like the way drinking loosened me up. I was much more outgoing and fun to be with, but I took it too far. After a while I only felt good when I had a few beers in me, so I was drinking way too much. Now I'm cutting back and forcing myself to try and be more confident without having to be drunk. It's hard work.

This is a very real danger of alcohol and drug use – the illusion of spontaneity and self-confidence in place of the real thing. Honest-to-goodness spontaneity and self-confidence take time and work, much of which happens during your teenage years. The illusion is seductive, but remember, it isn't real.

Another common reason for use is that it's considered glamorous. The message from society is twofold: on the one hand these substances are illegal, but on the other there's lots of hip media and advertising suggesting how cool you'll be if you use. Says Molly, 15:

> It's like you can't get away from the stuff. Half the billboards have all these gorgeous

people having a great time gathered around some
sort of booze or cigarette. After a while it
just wears on you. You begin to see yourself in
that situation — with these cool people having
a great time — even though you know it's just
advertising.

Another thing to remember is that adults are not exactly the best role
models. Frequently their motto is "do as I say, not as I do," as Jerry,
17, has found:

It isn't fair. If my parents have a rough week at
work they'll sit around and have a few drinks on
Friday night to relax into the weekend. But if I
have a rough week at school or in sports I can't
do the same. I'm expected to be responsible and
not drink, at least until I'm legal, when it
will be okay to have a few drinks after a rough
week at college or work.

Like it or not, you get lots of mixed messages about alcohol and drug
use. Taken to the extreme, you could make a solid intellectual argument either for or against use, but ultimately, the choice is yours, no
matter what society, parents, or friends do or say. There are basically
three options: no use, occasional use, and abuse. While there is a
clear line between no use and the other two options, the line between
occasional use and abuse is a lot harder to pin down.

Option #1: No use

Contrary to popular opinion, and as you may well know, not every
teenager uses alcohol or drugs. In fact, between 30% and 50% of you
never touch the stuff during high school, like Paige, 17:

It really pisses me off how so many people at
school assume that because I'm real social that
I drink. Far from it! The idea of getting drunk
and making a fool of myself is disgusting. Sure,
lots of my friends drink and smoke, and there's
a lot of alcohol at most parties, but still, I

never have. Friends who know me well understand this, but everyone else assumes the worst, even my parents.

There are lots of reasons why people choose not to use, including having felt the pain of addiction within their own home. Says Jenna, 17:

> My mother is an alcoholic. She has been on the wagon for a few years now — Alcoholics Anonymous meetings a few times a week. Things are better now, but when she was drinking things really sucked. My father left because of the drinking, and I used to have to put her to bed most nights. She used to drink and watch television until she fell asleep. Whenever she went out, which was rare, I was scared she would get into an accident — she has been arrested for drunk driving twice, and warned a bunch more times. So whenever I see a friend drinking I just shake my head. After how it has destroyed my mom's life I doubt I will ever try the stuff.

Or Shira, 15:

> My dad gets real mean when he's been drinking. If he gets the least bit angry he either hits one of us or throws things around the house, usually breaking something. And of course, if you try to point this out to him, it's like talking to a wall until he finally starts screaming, "Mind your own business!" I'm in no hurry to start drinking myself.

Others, like Nicole, 17, just aren't interested:

> There are lots of things I would rather do. Maybe in few years, probably when I get to college, I will start drinking. I just don't feel like it now.

Still others like Sierra, 16, are worried about their health and safety.

> I try to take good care of myself. I am a vege-
> tarian and play lots of sports, so it doesn't
> make sense for me to use drugs or alcohol.
> Besides, when my friends get drunk they do
> stupid things they wouldn't do if they were
> sober. Like sometimes they drive drunk and
> other times they have unprotected sex. Sure,
> when they're sober, they swear they'll never
> do these things, but as soon as they get a few
> beers in them they don't give it a second
> thought.

There are also those students like Ross, 16, who are interested but have decided to wait until they move away from home:

> Yeah, I am interested in trying alcohol, and
> maybe even some marijuana, but not until I leave
> home. My parents would die if they ever caught
> me. Besides, if I were to experiment now I would
> have to lie to my parents, and besides being a
> terrible liar, I hate lying to them. So it can
> wait a couple more years.

These are just a few of the reasons why students don't drink – there are certainly many more (just ask some of your classmates). The point to remember is that *should* you decide not to use, you won't be alone. That same decision is made by lots of your peers.

Option #2: Occasional use

There are actually two categories here: true-occasional users and regular-occasional users on the way to abuse. The true-occasional users only use periodically – depending on circumstances and mood – and have no pattern to how they use. Tamar, 17, is a true-occasional user:

> Sometimes I drink at parties and sometimes I get
> high with a few close friends. It really depends.
> I almost never plan to use ahead of time. And

lots of times, when others are getting drunk
or stoned I don't do either. I never party more
than once every couple of months.

The regular-occasional users have patterns to how they use, like at "most big parties," "Saturday nights with a couple of friends," or maybe "Tuesdays after school." Sound familiar? Patterns may range from a few times each month to less than once a month, depending on the person. Says Tim, 17:

The only times I get stoned are on weekend morn-
ings when me and a couple of buddies go hiking
on the edge of town — usually once a month or so,
and then only if I can count on coming home and
taking a nap.

Sometimes these people move into the gray area between occasional use and abuse, like Glenn, 16, did:

There are four of us that get together every
Thursday night for a few drinks. Actually, two
of the guys pretty much get plastered and me and
the other guy just have two or three beers. Then
we usually all party pretty hard on Friday night,
too. Saturday, well, it kind of depends if any
of us has a girlfriend or anything like that.

At this point, taking a closer look at substance use is in order.

So far we've discussed frequency of use, but still need to address quantity. The true-occasional user seldom gets drunk or stoned to the point where they use bad judgment (like driving under the influence or having unprotected sex) or get ill. Most importantly, they learn from their bad experiences, like Anya, 17, did:

I don't drink all that much, but there was
this one time that a bunch of us got real drunk
together. I mean real drunk. We had my friend's
house to ourselves, and after we drank the beer
we had bought we raided her parents' liquor

cabinet. To avoid getting caught we all had a
little of everything — vodka, gin, scotch, and
about ten other things. We all got pretty crazy,
but I drank way too much. And then I got real
sick. I was throwing up like crazy — I couldn't
stop myself, even when my stomach was emptied.
Then I passed out. My friends freaked out because
they couldn't wake me. They almost called 911,
but instead they took turns staying up with me,
checking my breathing and making sure I didn't
choke on my own vomit. It was all pretty nutty,
but, of course, I don't remember any of this
last part. But I do remember the headache and
body-ache I had for the next couple of days!
I didn't drink for a long time after that. Now,
when I do drink, which isn't that much, I stop
way before I get drunk. Once was enough, I hope.

Again, the ability to learn from your mistakes and adjust your behavior accordingly is a sign of a true-occasional user. Watch your own actions carefully.

Option #3: Abuse

Then there are the people who use despite continued, negative consequences to themselves. Rather than learn from their mistakes, abusers minimize the effects of their use, like Todd, 17, did:

I got pretty buzzed the other night. When I was
driving home I spaced for a second and hit the
wheel on the curb. There was no damage to anything other than a flat tire. I fixed it and drove
home without a problem. It was no big deal.

Or Stephanie, 15:

It seems that every time I get drunk I end up
getting together with this one guy. Usually we
end up having sex — and, no, we don't use protection. I know it's stupid, but we just can't help

ourselves. It's like our true feelings come out
when we're loaded, but when we see each other at
school it's like nothing ever happened.

Neither of these people learned from their mistakes. The substance dominated their judgment both when they used *and* when they thought about their past use, which is why you feel like you are talking to a brick wall if you confront someone like this. The thinking and behavior of the abuser gets taken over by the cycle and, as a result, they will downplay everything you say, make fun of you for being so straight, or get angry and suggest you mind your own business. Liza, 16, has experienced this firsthand:

When I tried talking to Shawna about her getting
high all the time she just laughed in my face.
Then she got real defensive and told me to
mind my own business. It was like there was no
way she was going to hear what I had to say. I
dropped it after that. I mean, what's the sense?

Even though it's tough, it's important to raise your concerns to the person you think is abusing. It will be an awkward conversation, but it's important to persevere because in the end it might save you both from a lot of grief. (See the next chapter on Helping Friends, beginning on page 54, for more on this.)

The unfairness of addictions

The path from occasional use to abuse is different for everybody, as everybody has a different sensitivity to alcohol and drugs. In this respect, we all have to face the harsh reality that addictions aren't fair. One person can go from casual experimentation to abuse and addiction after only a few times of use, while for another it might take years and years of steady use to cover the same distance. This is a genetics issue, over which you have no control. For example:

• If one of your parents is an alcoholic, then you are 34% more likely to be an alcoholic than the average person.

- If both parents are alcoholics, then you are 400% more likely to be an alcoholic than the average person.
- If you are male and both your father and his father are alcoholics, then you are 900% more likely to be an alcoholic than the average person.

And you should realize that intelligence is no protection from addiction. In fact, it might have the opposite effect – for example, physicians are eight times more likely to be addicts than the average person, and six times more likely to be alcoholics than the average person. Members of the elite MENSA group (IQ of 140 just to qualify to take their entrance test!) have the highest addiction and alcoholic rates of any other group of people. Again, it's important to know yourself, and to be aware of your habits and patterns. (All these statistics are taken from *Uppers, Downers, and All-Arounders* by Daryl Inaba and William Cohen.)

Health and safety

You won't find too many doctors or scientists who can claim that alcohol and drugs are good for you – at least not on the level that vegetables and whole grains are good for you. To use or not use is your decision and responsibility, and you will feel, more than anyone else, the consequences of this choice. Whatever you choose, there are some safety requirements and health concerns that you need to consider. Jody, 16, addresses one of them:

> I go out with a few of my friends drinking every month or so. We never plan it, it just sort of happens. So sometimes things get a little hairy. You know, we're all pretty drunk and nobody can drive. Usually, whoever claims she is the soberest ends up driving, but most of the time none of us is very sober.

Or Sean, 16, brings up another:

> We were both a little high and one thing led to another. And just because neither of us had a

condom wasn't enough to stop us. It isn't like
we planned on having sex. We just did it.

Whether it's about safe sex, designated drivers, and drug or alcohol use, you have to learn to be responsible about being irresponsible. It will save lots of pain and agony in the long run, and maybe even a life or two. Consider it common sense, not a moral issue, and as LeVonne, 16, found out, you might even be in for a pleasant surprise or two:

A bunch of us got really drunk at a party the
other night. None of us could drive, but of
course the guy with the car was convinced that
he was fine. He wasn't. No way I was getting in
that car. [I tried taking my buddy's keys away
but there was no way.] But when I went back to
the party I realized there was nobody I knew
well enough to ask for a ride. Well, my mom has
always told me to call if I needed a ride — she
promised no questions. So I took a deep breath
and called her. She was asleep so it took a
while for her to understand. Finally, she came
and got me. When I got in the car I could tell
she was pissed, but then she just sort of smiled
and told me to buckle my seat belt. At breakfast
the next day she told me how proud she was of me
for calling, and how angry she was at me for
lying — I had told her I was going to the movies.
I ended up having to do chores for a couple
of hours around the house (with a splitting
headache), but afterwards she took me out for
a great lunch. She was pretty cool.

Obviously LeVonne has a really understanding and trusting mother, but even if you don't, your safety is your responsibility. Whether it's driving drunk, using unknown drugs, or having sex under the influence, the safety decisions are up to you. Be wise.

This helps you understand the differences between occasional use and abuse in your life. For each category, describe what you might use, where you might use and under what circumstances, and how much you'd use.

Occasional use

What?

Where and under what circumstances?

How much?

Abuse

What?

Where and under what circumstances?

How much?

MORE READING:

Uppers, Downers, and All-Arounders by Daryl Inaba and William Cohen.

8
helping friends and yourself

There are two ways of exerting one's strength:
one is pushing down, the other is pulling up.
                    Booker T. Washington

Sometimes the things our parents most fear for us turn up in a friend – I'm talking here about addictions, pregnancy, eating disorders, depression, or suicidal thoughts. These situations are tough on your friend, and he or she needs your support, but they're also tough on you. If you find yourself in this position, there are a few things to remember.

First, there's not much you can do to bring about a quick solution. Just as the problem took awhile to develop, it won't go away over night. It takes lots of time just to understand what's going on, much less solve it, as Jeff, 16, found out:

> I had no idea things were so bad with his family, so when he started talking about how cool it would be to commit suicide I didn't know what to say. At that point I was more worried about saying the wrong thing than anything else. It was much more complicated than wanting to die or to live.

54

Secondly, and to state a tricky thing as simply as possible, there are two kinds of personal problems in the world: those that can be solved with better information, and those that require time, support, and commitment to the person's well-being. (This section addresses the latter.) This means that at some point in the life of the problem you may have to go against your friend's wishes in the interest of her well-being. Listen to Celeste, 16:

> Melinda made me promise, and I stupidly agreed, not to tell her parents about all the speed she was using. But when it got so bad that she wasn't sleeping or eating, I decided I had to tell them before she died or something. When I told her I was telling them she called me every name in the book, but I didn't see any other choice. What if she overdosed?

Thirdly, bear in mind that it's impossible for you to fully understand your friend's problem. Andrea, 15, doesn't share the same understanding of the issues as her friend does, but she can still try to see how her friend views the problem:

> It really doesn't make any sense to me. Sure, I want to be thin and all that, but there's no way I would starve myself to the point of being all skin and bones. I don't have the discipline for that, and besides, it's just not that important to me.

Still, listening to and trying to understand your friend remains one of the most critical and powerful ways you can support her. Let's take a look at some of the big problems that can happen during high school (but remember that this is only a partial list).

Suicide

Teen suicide feels more common than it actually is because of all the publicity it attracts. Currently, about 1 in 10,000 teenagers commits suicide each year – but that number is on the rise. When a teenager commits suicide, it represents a failure of our society in the worst way – a youth, our hope for the future, has given up. Additionally, the effects are felt quite deeply by the school community, which includes many more people and closer relationships than the communities of most adults. It's important to understand that the threat to commit suicide – where the person has a plan, the means, and a clear intention to kill themselves – is very different from having passing thoughts about suicide, which, as scary as it may sound, most everybody has at some point. Tony, 17, clarifies the difference:

> Yeah, sure, I've thought about suicide a few times. I think everybody does. It's scary to think about, but with all that's happening to me it would be weird to not even consider it. But there's a big difference between thinking and doing, and I know I would never do it.

So the first question you want to consider in trying to help a friend is *is this a serious thought or just a passing idea?* You can get a sense of this in two ways – by listening and by asking questions. First, listen to everything they say. If your friend is serious, they will probably have ideas about how to actually kill themselves, how it will affect their family and friends, and what they should write in their suicide note. Jasmine, 15, has been through this with her friend Celia:

> Listening to Celia made me even more scared than when she just mentioned killing herself. She had it all planned out in her head: she knew where her father kept his gun and bullets, and had even written a draft of her suicide note. She wanted to know what I thought of the note!

The second thing you need to do is get past your fear of talking about suicide, and start asking questions. Most people who talk to somebody about their suicidal thoughts don't want to go through with it; in a backwards sort of way, they're asking for help. (Think about it: if someone were 100% sure they wanted to commit suicide, they wouldn't talk to anybody about it, they'd just do it.) So ask them why they want to. Ask them if they have a plan and what it is. Ask them when they plan to do it. The harder it is for them to answer, then, generally, the safer they are. Jack, 16, was able to discern the difference with his friend, Andy:

> When I asked Andy how he planned to kill himself, he had a few different ideas but he was pretty vague. After awhile it became clear that he was just beginning to entertain the idea, but seemed a ways away from making a decision one way or the other.

This is not to underestimate the severity of just considering suicide, and in fact, there's no 100% guaranteed way to determine how serious someone is about following through. They may not have a detailed plan when you talk to them, and yet still kill themselves that night. This is not to scare you, but rather just to remind you that there's no guarantee, which brings up the last and most important point: before you leave them alone, get them to promise that they won't hurt themselves without talking to you again. Or, get them to promise not to hurt themselves for some specified amount of time – say 24 hours. While this is still no guarantee, it's the best you can do. And, make sure they sound believable to you, as Sheri, 15, did:

> I made Sam tell me that he wasn't going to kill himself without talking to me first a bunch of times. I just didn't trust the way he said it the first few times. He needed to see I was real serious and real scared.

If you have a friend who is seriously considering suicide, it will undoubtedly dominate your life until the threat passes, as it did for Christa, 16:

> When Richard was starting to cut his legs and threatening to cut his wrists it made me crazy. I felt like I had to check in with him all the time. And since I was the only one he told about this, I felt personally responsible for him. If he killed himself I knew I would feel like it was my fault.

When you find yourself in a situation like this, it's useful to imagine how you will feel if your friend does kill himself, as weird as that may seem. This future thinking can help you figure out what to do in the present, as can talking it out with other people. Phil, 17, used the latter strategy:

> After awhile I couldn't take the tension of Corey's constant talk about suicide, so I went and talked to one of my teachers about it. [I made sure not to use her name, just in case he would have to tell somebody.] He was helpful to talk to, and I talked to him for a few minutes just about every day for the next couple of weeks. While I supported Corey, he supported me. I was actually surprised that he was that helpful.

So did Jackie, 16:

> When I couldn't take it anymore I went and told the school counselor what was going on with Russell. She helped me a lot — both in feeling better about myself and in figuring out what to do. In the end she met with both Russell and me to talk about how he felt. At first he was pretty angry with me for telling her, but that didn't last long at all. I think he was actually glad to have someone to talk to who could really help him.

Talking to someone else can certainly help *you* cope with your friend's situation, and will probably also help your friend as you are better equipped to help them.

While helping a friend like this, you may also find yourself experiencing all sorts of unusual thoughts in your head, like Shirley, 15, did:

> On the one hand I was scared that she would kill herself, but on the other, I was angry because part of me felt that she was just doing this to get attention. I know that sounds awful, but that's what I thought sometimes.

If you can relate to what Shirley is saying, don't worry. As strange as it sounds, most of what you feel and think during situations like this is probably partly true, even if your thoughts and feelings seem to contradict one another. This is why it's important to find someone to talk with; you aren't an expert on suicide, so find someone who is! Every city and county has an anonymous Suicide Hot Line – look in your local phone book or call information – and you shouldn't hesitate to call if you need some help with your friend. Listen to what they say and then combine it with your knowledge of your friend, and follow through on what you believe is the best course of action. This might involve telling your friend's parents or it might mean not telling anyone and handling it yourself. You have to decide and you *can* make a good decision, just make sure you consult with other people before doing so, like Lucy, 15, did:

> When I called the Suicide Hot Line they asked
> me all sorts of questions that I would never
> have thought of. After awhile they told me that
> it was probably nothing to worry about yet,
> but that if she kept on talking about it then
> I should call back to figure out what to do
> next.

And Stan, 16:

> When I told the woman on the hot line what my
> friend had already said and done she got real
> concerned and told me that my friend was in real
> danger of seriously hurting or killing himself.
> Then she walked me through, step-by-step, some
> of the options I had, and she didn't pressure me
> one way or the other – the final decision was
> mine. Thankfully it all worked out, but there
> sure were a few rough spots there. Over the
> course of that week I must have talked to that
> woman for ten hours!

One final word. If someone you know or someone in your school commits suicide, then that person and the tragedy will get lots of attention. Newspapers and television stations will give numerous detailed reports about the victim's life, family, friends, and activities, focusing almost completely on the positive aspects. The person becomes sort of famous – albeit after they're dead, and much too late for them to appreciate it. Don't be fooled into thinking that this is a good way to get attention, because it's not. Some kids who are considering suicide as an escape to their pain can get seduced over the edge by all the attention and media coverage the victim gets. Remember, if there's a suicide in your community, make sure to take care of yourself and keep an eye on your friends – everyone is more vulnerable after a suicide has happened. And finally, some words from a survivor of a suicide attempt. Annie, 17, adds this:

Last spring was a very difficult time for me. I was plagued by debilitating migraine headaches which kept me out of school. The headaches were made worse by stress and a vicious cycle developed. The more school that I missed, the more stressed out I got, and the more migraines I suffered. Coupled with other family stresses, it got to the point on April 22 where I felt that I had no future to look forward to, and I tried to kill myself.

I didn't really want to die, I just wanted to stop living in the same painful way that I had been for the past few months. I left school the day that I attempted suicide smiling, a mask I suppose for the pain I didn't even know I was feeling. My decision to kill myself was not planned or premeditated, it was impulsive and took place only moments before my attempt. I had a migraine at the time, and I took some of my prescribed medication. It did nothing to help the pain so I took some more, by which time I was pretty out of it. Although I knew I had finally had enough, I kept taking the medication, overdosing with the intention of killing myself. In my case, as in many cases, the drugs that I took affected my judgment.

I'm telling you today about my suicide attempt
as a context for the realizations that I had when I
woke up alive and found that I was still in a world
I had intended to leave. I don't want to focus on
the details of the attempt because attempting
suicide was only the manifestation of problems
I was forced to deal with afterward.

I also wanted you to see that you don't have
to be crazy or repressed or depressed all the
time to attempt suicide. You just have to be in
the habit of not dealing with your pain. I think
that one of the biggest mistakes we make in this
world is assuming that we all have to be happy
all the time. That's totally unnatural, not to
mention impossible to do. It's normal to have
pain, and you have to let yourself be open to it
because if you go around all tense all the time,
trying to keep the pain away, you'll never be
able to experience the happiness because you
won't be open to the world.

Addictions and eating disorders

Addictions are really not all that different from eating disorders –
they're both compulsive, self-destructive behaviors. Both are capa-
ble of slowly, but surely, taking over the victims' minds. If you have a
friend suffering from some sort of addiction or eating disorder, you
need to be especially aware of this fact. Listen to what Daria, 15, says
about her disorder:

I know it's strange to say, but it's like bulimia
is my friend — maybe even my best friend. I think
bulimic thoughts all the time. Even when other
friends express concern for me I can hear the
bulimia making fun of them so that I don't take
what they say seriously.

Or Steve, 17:

The only time I feel good about myself is when

I'm drunk or stoned. It's like all my problems
just go away and I can finally let loose and be
myself.

People with eating disorders have an irresistible urge not to eat –
hard to imagine for those of us who have trouble sticking to a diet!
Your job as a friend is to offer support while ignoring the disease, as
Sheila, 16, did:

I learned early on that there was nothing I
could do to get my anorexic friend to eat. Even
though I tried baking cookies and bringing extra
sandwiches, none of it worked. Then I realized
it was like two people living in her body – the
Jan I knew and the anorexic Jan. So I decided
to only pay attention to the Jan I knew. I told
her I was concerned about her health and her
not eating, but that I wouldn't bring it up with
her anymore after this. Then, as hard as it was,
I never mentioned it again. I just worked on
reaching out and talking to the Jan that was my
friend, not the anorexic Jan. I wasn't going to
let that disease take away my friend!

I have dealt with many students with eating disorders, and watched
them fight back. What follows is a long letter that I once sent to a student suffering from anorexia. It offers a good summary of how and
why eating disorders take over the victims' minds.

Dear Ava,
From our conversation, it's clear that you
are now making a stand against the tyranny of
anorexia in your life. You also understand that
this is both a long and difficult process. To
this extent, you need all the support you can
get, which also means understanding, on a deep
level, what actually supports you as a person
and what supports the anorexia's mind control.
You have discovered that this is not as obvious
as it seems.

Your parents. Clearly you want their full support, but past efforts have failed to claim it. You have insisted on nonfat foods, avoided family obligations that centered on dining, exercised fanatically within their plain view, and have still not gotten the attention you need from them. Further, you visited a physician in an attempt to get the subject out in the open with your parents, but that failed miserably as all he did was focus on the vegetarianism and refer you to a nutritionist — as if you need any outside assistance in monitoring your eating habits!

Even though your skin is slightly jaundiced, your wrists are tiny, your hair is beginning to fall out, and you have lost twenty pounds over the past six months, nobody seems willing to recognize what's going on. They all want to look the other way in the hopes that it's "just a phase." This may have been true in the beginning, but you are now way beyond the beginning! On top of this, what attention your parents have paid to the anorexia has resulted in a bunch of mixed messages: Your mom upset with your exclusively nonfat diet on the one hand and yelling at you for eating a taco with cheese and sour cream on the other. Your dad worried about the amount of exercising you are doing and yet complimenting you on how good you look. (Sadly, you have recognized how "thin beauty" has taken over the typical American mind — especially with men.)

You fear that if you do muster the strength to fully name the anorexia in front of your parents that you will inadvertently invite them in as "food monitors," a possibility that you dread. In this, you really warmed to what happened with Karen and her anorexia. Once it was recognized, she started seeing a therapist and her physician. The therapist was someone she liked and with whom she simply talked about her life's events and seldom directly discussed food. The physician she met with asked only about the anorexia. He was very firm and had a clear weight in mind, and, if Karen dropped to that weight, he would automatically place her in the hospital for at least a month, and Karen knew he was not kidding. Furthermore, you especially liked that he forbade her family, and especially her parents, to ever talk to her about food or anorexia. In fact, he insisted that Karen eat what, where, and when she like. Her parents could never insist that she join them for dinner, or any other meal. Only he, the physician, would discuss food and eating with her. And yes, this was the person with whom she was angry, rude, and outspoken, all without feeling guilty!

Your friends. You need them now more than ever, but you understand how hard it is for them. The anorexia, by gradually taking over your thinking, has created a fog all around you that leaves you a step behind in conversations and in understanding what is happening around you. In fact, the coldness of the fog encourages you to retreat further into your own world and the world of anorexia, which is compulsive in its focus on food, grams of fat, calories, and future planning for food. However, much to the credit of your friends, once they got over their shyness about the food and focused on their concern for you, they were supportive. While you did not like them offering you food and encouraging you to eat, you did appreciate their intentions. And you understand why, with no results, they stopped offering the encouragement. You felt somewhat abandoned but not able to tell them clearly what you needed: their

unconditional love and support throughout this
ordeal, even though they would not be able to
directly help or make you better. If only you
could have gotten them to see anorexia as a kind
of long-term pneumonia. Anyway, they have gotten
discouraged, and with the distancing effects
of the anorexia they have drifted away from you.
Though you know it isn't too late, it will
take time and effort to bring them back into
your life.

Your teachers. Oddly, this has been the best
support system you have had to date. Unexpect-
edly, Mrs. Nelson recognized what was going on
with you and spoke her concerns and support to
you directly. It was a great relief for someone
to recognize what was happening without your
having to tell them. Further, she was not afraid
to talk about it with you and seemed very understanding and nonjudgmental. In fact, it was the
relationship with her that encouraged you to
squarely address the anorexia by coming to my
office to get some ideas and help. Quite a
big step.

We left our conversation off with the idea of
deciding how to alert your parents to the situation without further strengthening the hold of
anorexia. We discussed several options: having
you write them a letter (as conversations often
don't go as planned); inviting them into my
office and having you tell them here; or inviting
them into my office, without you, and having _me_
catch them up for you. It's now in your hands.
While you want all the support you can get, you
also fully understand that only you can make
this stand against anorexia. You call the shots
as to when, where, and how.

    See you soon. Mike

Whatever the addiction might be, the points to keep in mind are similar:

- Directly voice your concerns to your friend, but don't expect them to really hear you.
- Support your friend as a person, regardless of the addiction.
- Learn more about what your friend is dealing with through agencies in your city or town, teachers or counselors at school, and books.
- Look out for your friend's welfare in terms of health and safety – things like drinking and driving.
- If you feel like your friend is in too deep and can no longer properly recognize and deal with the problem, think seriously about telling his or her parents what's going on.

One final point: don't give up on your friend. Confronting an addiction or eating disorder takes time and effort; it won't happen over night. For instance, Ava (for whom the letter was written) is doing very well these days. Sure, she's always vulnerable to a relapse in times of huge stress, but she also has many more tools at her disposal now. Basically, she's normal and happy, so hang in there with your friend and they'll get there, too.

Pregnancy

Pregnancy is very *very* different from the two problems discussed so far. Unlike suicide there's (usually) no decision made about getting pregnant. And unlike addictions or eating disorders, it's a one-time thing, rather than an ongoing process (although the net result can be quite permanent). If a friend gets pregnant, your job is to help her figure out what to do and support her in following through with her decision. Stephanie, 16, talks about what it's like to find out that a friend is pregnant:

> It really threw me when Celeste said she was
> pregnant. I didn't know what to say. My first
> question was so stupid. "How did it happen?" And
> then, "Are you sure?" But what really threw me

was that she wanted my help in figuring out what
to do while I still hadn't gotten used to the
fact that she was pregnant. She had known for a
day, but this was the first I had heard about it
or even her suspicion of being pregnant.

Stephanie was shocked and surprised, but Celeste clearly needed help
with her obvious first decision – whether or not to have the baby.
Josh, 17, helped his friends Phil and Elisa with a similar question:

When Phil told me that Elisa was pregnant I was
surprised, but not shocked. I knew they weren't
being too careful with birth control. Phil was
pretty sure he wanted Elisa to have an abortion,
but he wanted her to make the decision. He said
he would support her no matter what she decided,
which kind of surprised me because Phil is
not that responsible a guy. We ended up talking
a lot over the next few days while they made
a decision about what to do. In our talks he
wanted to explore both options: having the baby
and having an abortion. They ended up having an
abortion.

In this case, a decision was made to have an abortion; the next step is
to find out where, when, and how. This is where friends play a vital
role. During this process, you have to be commited to helping your
friend regardless of your own opinion. You should make your views
known, but be careful not to push the issue as it's clearly not your decision. Melody, 16, discusses what it's like to disagree with your
friend's decision:

Kelly kept wanting to know what I would do in her
shoes, but whenever I told her, it was usually
the opposite of what she wanted to do. I think
she just needed an opinion to bounce ideas off
of. It felt good to tell her what I thought
so that I could support her in what she decided
to do.

Choosing an abortion usually means a trip to Planned Parenthood or other similar agency. (To find out about abortion services where you live, call the National Abortion Federation Hot Line at (800) 223-0618.) Most people like company on this first visit, so you should offer to go with them, but it's obviously their choice. This first visit is usually just for getting information, but not always – it depends on where you live. Damon, 16, says:

> When we went to Planned Parenthood they told us
> up front that if Diana wanted to make the deci-
> sion to get an abortion today that was fine,
> but she couldn't get the actual abortion today.
> They make you set a date for the abortion so you
> really have to think it through to make sure it's
> something you want to do. Once you have the
> abortion there's no changing your mind.

The next big decision is about whether or not to tell parents. Some states actually require parental permission for an abortion if the woman is under a certain age; you should call Planned Parenthood to find out the specific details. Having the support and understanding of parents is a big plus, but the fear is that in telling them, they might try to make the decision themselves. Says Betty, 17:

> Sheri was sure she didn't want her parents to
> know, but I still asked her about it. If it were
> me I would want my parents to know. In the end
> I realized she was right; I don't think her
> parents would have handled it well.

Support your friend's decision about telling her parents, no matter what *you* might do.

When the day finally arrives, offer to accompany her to the abortion – if nothing else be sure to pick her up afterwards. This is when the second half of your work as a friend kicks in – dealing with the emotional aftermath of the abortion. Read the chapter on Loss and Grief for more about this (beginning on page 110) as your friend will go through all those feelings many times over. She needs your understanding and presence more now than ever. Carie, 16, helped her friend, Fran:

```
After the abortion Fran wanted me around a lot,
even though we hardly talked about it. Usually
she just wanted to listen to music together
or go for walks. I think she was scared to be
alone. And sometimes she just cried while I
held her.
```

Finally, and at the great risk of stating the obvious, don't divulge what your friend tells you. If you leak word of her abortion, it will ruin your friendship and leave her feeling totally vulnerable and unable to trust. If you've had trouble keeping secrets in the past, now is the time to learn.

Now suppose your friend decides to have the baby. Says Cara, 16:

```
I never thought about what I would do if I got
pregnant until I got pregnant. I guess I always
imagined that I would get an abortion. But the
idea of another person inside me just blows me
away. So a couple of nights ago I told my parents
I was pregnant — we've talked a lot since then.
I've decided to keep the baby, and they're will-
ing to help out. The only thing left to do is to
tell the father.
```

Obviously, there's no hiding the decision to have the baby; eventually everyone will know. This is good, as it will enable more people to support your friend besides just you, but it also raises other questions, such as whether she'll keep the baby or put it up for adoption. If she keeps it, how will she care for it? Can her parents help out or can she afford to hire child care? Will she stay in school? There are lots of issues to wrestle with, which is why your friend needs your help, like Monica, 17, did:

```
Once I decided to have and keep the baby myself
there were all these other decisions I had to
make. Everyone was great — even though my parents
were real angry at first, they got into it by the
time the baby was born. My mom even volunteered
to take care of the baby while I was at school,
and school changed my schedule so I could get
```

out early every day. My friends were great too.
I needed to talk a lot about what was happening, and what was so great was that while
everyone had different ideas about what I
should do, they all still supported me in what
I decided.

Keeping a baby requires particularly long-term support from friends.
In fact, the teenage mother's situation changes so much that it becomes difficult for her to be part of regular high school life. Tiffany,
16, knows what this feels like:

After Zach was born I felt like I had no life. I
came home after lunch and cared for him all day.
Then at night I tried to keep up with my homework. Then the next day it was the same thing.
I completely lost touch with my friends, I just
didn't have time for them anymore. They still
came by and everything, but we just didn't have
that much in common anymore. I mean taking care
of a baby and trying to get a date for prom
don't have a lot in common.

So clearly your friend is going to need lots of love and support.
And what about the father in all this? Usually the teenage father's
role varies, depending upon the couple's relationship before the
pregnancy. Were they in a committed relationship or had they just
met? Was it just a fling between them? The answers to these questions will give you some idea of what to expect, but even if they were
in a committed relationship the pregnancy is sure to test their bond.
Diana, 17, talks about her friend's situation:

Teddy was wonderful when Cheryl got pregnant.
They had been going out for over a year and were
really into each other. In fact, he really wanted
to marry her. But that was way too much for her.
She wasn't ready for marriage, never mind a baby.
When she decided to get an abortion it got ugly
between them. After the abortion they stayed

together for a short while, but eventually they
drifted. They were just never the same.

Justine's friend Sylvia, 16, had a much different experience:

It was awful, as soon as he found out that Sylvia
was pregnant he didn't want anything to do with
her. He even told her that he had been meaning
to break up with her for awhile anyway. Then he
just began to ignore her, like maybe she would
just go away. I think that was harder for her
than getting pregnant.

In both these cases, a real relationship had been established well before the pregnancy. In less committed situations, the father is usually
even more unpredictable. Says Laura, 15:

He was such a jerk. Not only did he not support
her but he spread rumors around that it wasn't
even his kid!

And Beth, 16:

When she told him she was pregnant they talked
a long time. Finally he said he would help with
whatever she wanted to do — he would pay for half
the abortion if she wanted or would help support
the baby with whatever money he could if she
decided to have the baby. I never would have
expected this of him either, I thought he would
have been the kind of guy who would have just
walked away.

The bottom line is that since the father's reaction can vary so greatly,
your friend definitely needs your consistent support.

Suppose the problem is yours?

If you're the one pregnant, addicted, having suicidal thoughts, or
suffering from an eating disorder, then there are a few things to keep
in mind. First of all, don't think that if you ignore the problem it will

go away. Realize that you're neither the first nor last person to have this problem, and that there's lots of help out there. Granted, you probably never expected to be dealing with this, but you are. As Kelly, 15, points out, recognizing the problem can be half the battle:

> For a long time my friends told me that I was too skinny and that I should eat more, but I never took them seriously. It felt good to have them say that. I was sure that I didn't have a problem with food or eating. It was only when my skin started to turn yellow that I began to believe that I had a problem.

The next really important thing to do is to find someone you can talk to. You don't need a professional problem-solver, just someone you feel comfortable talking with. It will really help you sort through all your confusion, as Devon, 15, found out:

> Talking with Ann was so helpful. Just her listening to what I was thinking about and then asking questions helped me to better understand what was going on.

And Bruce, 16:

> Mr. Delstin was wonderful. He couldn't tell me what to do but he helped me understand what was going on. Then he helped me figure out where to go to get the help I needed. He didn't solve my problem, only I could do that.

Finally, go the distance of seeking out and using any resources available in your community, as Marissa, 16, did:

> When I finally realized I was hooked on pot my friend Steve was great to talk with. Not only that, but he told me about Narcotics Anonymous, which really helped.

And Naomi, 15:

> Tianna was great to talk to about my feelings of
> hopelessness and death. She even went through
> the Yellow Pages with me until we found a Sui-
> cide Hot Line for me to call. She stayed in my
> room with me for the first few calls, just to
> make sure I felt comfortable with the person I
> was talking to. I don't know if I would have
> made it without her.

There's no need to be selfish about the problems you're having. Let your friends (and parents or teachers when appropriate) help you, as they are your best and first source of support. In fact, letting them help you will even bring you closer together. Remember, there's no reason to suffer alone.

THINK ABOUT IT

The purpose here is to help you realize what you already do when faced with a problem.

1. Briefly describe a tough problem you had in the past.

2. How did you handle it? If you sought advice, where did you find it? What was useful and what wasn't? Who was helpful and who wasn't?

3. Looking back at that incident, do you think there's anything you could have done differently? What would you recommend to a friend in a similar situation?

4. Why do you think you didn't handle it that way in the first place? Lack of information? Lack of a friend? Some type of fear?

MORE READING:

The Power to Prevent Suicide: A Guide For Teens Helping Teens by Richard E. Nelson, Ph.D., and Judith C. Galas.

Teens with AIDS Speak Out by Mary Kittredge.

Surviving Teen Pregnancy by Shirley Arthur.

Teenage Fathers by Karen Gravelle and Leslie Peterson.

race, gender, and economics

9

Classism and greed are making
insignificant all other kinds of isms.
Ruby Dee

The Declaration of Independence states that, "All men are created equal," and while this is true, it's also true that not all people are *treated* equally. More importantly, it fails to consider how race, gender, and economics affect how you live your life and the decisions you make. Anita, 15, talks about how economics have affected her friendships:

> I had the same three best friends through most
> of middle school. They were all from rich fami-
> lies. I was not, but that never made a differ-
> ence to our friendship. But then in high school,
> when they all got fancy computers and started
> going on ski trips, I started to feel left out.
> There was no way my family could afford all
> those things. At first I got angry at my parents—
> later I was even embarrassed by them. But finally
> it was just too much, and I gradually stopped

75

spending so much time with them. They're still
friends of mine, but not best friends.

Like it or not, these issues do influence your choice in friends, activities, and beliefs. Since everyone wants to be accepted, it makes sense (and is generally easier) to hang out with people who are similar to you, as Marie, 17, points out:

> The friends I hung around with during freshman
> year were all just like me — we wore the same
> kinds of clothes, did the same things, and yes,
> we were all the same race. Now [a senior] I have
> lots of different kinds of friends, but back
> then I think it was just easier that way.

Sometimes, you have to spend some time figuring out how these things influence you before you can do anything about them. Says Lindsy, 15:

> My family is comfortable, but definitely not
> rich. But a couple of my friends come from real
> wealthy families. At first I never invited them
> over, because I was too embarrassed. But after
> my parents started bugging me about it I started
> having them come over more often. Now it's no
> big deal, but it was hard at first. And it has
> led to some weird conversations — like they
> couldn't believe that we don't have our own
> washer and dryer, or that we rent our house.

And James, 15:

> At my school the black, Asian, Mexican, and
> white students all have areas where they hang
> out. Generally not too many people cross over
> these areas — at least not in public. But that
> seemed stupid to me, so lately I have been going
> out of my way to cross over as much as possible.
> It's hard though, because at first everyone is
> suspicious of what I'm doing.

Once you're aware of the fact that race, economics, and gender influence the world, then you start seeing subtle things you never noticed before. It's these barely noticeable things that are frequently the most powerful, but once you see them you can never *not* see them again, as Rosie, 16, points out:

> In our history class the teacher was talking
> about how girls are treated differently in class
> than boys. I really argued with her about this.
> I think the teachers at this school try hard
> to treat everyone the same. But after that I
> started watching more closely. Just about every
> time a guy and a girl had their hand up to answer
> a question, the guy got called on. In fact, much
> of the time the guys just yelled the answer out
> and never got yelled at. One time a girl did
> this, and she got cut off by the teacher for
> talking out of turn. And the really strange part
> is that it didn't matter if the teacher was male
> or female!

Learning to recognize these issues – and your response to them – is invaluable. One thing most people come to realize as they address all this is how much of it comes from your family and the way you were raised. As Lisa, 15, says:

> People are always telling me how amazing I am in
> terms of speaking out. Actually, what's amazing
> to them is not that I'm speaking out, it's that
> I'm a girl who speaks out. But they don't under-
> stand that that's how I was raised. My mom never
> shies away from anything.

Or Shannon, 16:

> My mother and father never knew anyone Asian
> when they were kids, so when I started dating
> an Asian guy it took them a long time to get used
> to the idea. They were pretty racist at first in
> what they expected, but they got over it, slowly.

Clearly, stereotypes are everywhere, and one very common one is gender. Popular books today describe females as more relationship-oriented and males as more task-oriented. While this is generally true, it's also important to realize that there are usually as many exceptions to the rule as there are adherents, so prepare for everything. The same is true for race and economics. The key is to avoid stereotypes whenever possible, and it's really *always* possible.

THINK ABOUT IT

Compared to the others in this book, these questions might seem a little more uncomfortable. If you find yourself getting angry, take a deep breath and try to see what's behind the anger, as it usually covers deeper, more vulnerable emotions.

Race

Imagine that you have just gotten romantically involved with a person from another race.

1. How would your friends react?

2. How would your parents and family react?

3. How would strangers react if they saw you walking down the street holding hands? How would you react to their reactions?

Gender

1. List the advantages and disadvantages to being female.

2. List the advantages and disadvantages to being male.

3. If you could have chosen to be either a boy or girl, which would you have picked? Why?

MORE READING:

Children of Promise: African American Literature and Art For Young People by Charles Sullivan (Editor).

Speaking Out: Teenagers Talk on Race, Sex, and Identity by Susan Kukin.

Respecting Our Differences: A Guide To Getting Along In A Changing World by Lynn Duvall.

10
parents

*If I had two lives I would give you
(parents) one. But I only have one.
Simone Weil*

If your relationship with your parents hasn't already changed, it will soon – there's just no way it can remain the same since *you* are changing so much. Ideally, your parents have either already given you, or will soon begin to give you, more freedom and power in your life, and in return you will assume more responsibility for yourself. Says Chris, 16:

> My parents are pretty cool. They understand that
> I don't want to talk to them as much as I did
> when I was a kid. And they let me make lots of
> my own decisions. Sure, sometimes we yell at
> one another, but overall things are pretty good
> between us. At least they don't try to run my
> life like some of my friends' parents.

If your parents don't support your independence then you have one of two choices: either go along with them and wait until you move away from home, or, go underground (as it were) and tell them what they want to hear but do whatever you want. Neither of these options is very satisfying or useful in the long run. If you simply let them run your life, then your "decision-making muscles" never develop. Belinda, 18, experienced just this:

> When I went off to college it was totally wild. All through high school my parents kept me on a short leash, so when I was finally off on my own I went overboard. It was a lot of fun at first, but by the end of first semester I was flunking out. I just had to try all the things my parents never let me do — I stayed out late, got drunk, skipped classes, and did all sorts of things I could never do at home. It was weird, I got drunk with freedom.

On the other hand, if you simply go underground, it's just a matter of time before you get caught and everything comes crashing down. And even if you never *do* get caught, the constant lying forms a barrier between you and your parents, which cuts you off from their support. Craig, 16, found this out:

> My parents are control freaks. They want to know everything I do and think about. I try to avoid them, but when they corner me I usually just lie to them. The only time I regret lying to them is when I need them. Sometimes I just need them to understand or even talk to, but that would mean telling them the truth about a lot of other things besides whatever is bothering me. So I just keep it to myself.

Neither the controlling nor lying relationship is very satisfying – to either you or your parents. Listen to how some parents feel about this, like Linda, 44:

> I feel like such a nag with my teenager, but I don't know what else to do. I can't pretend that her constant talking on the phone, not doing her homework, or cryptic responses to my questions

doesn't bother and concern me. What am I supposed
to do, just let her fall apart? I know she needs
to do it for herself, but I can't stand being
helpless.

And Nina, 42:

My son and I have a horrible relationship. I
know he lies to me all the time. But what's
really sick is that I don't call him on it, I
just let it go. I don't want to be in his face
all the time, so I'm just hoping he can handle
it and doesn't get himself into too much trouble.
I don't like the way I'm handling it, but I want
him to like me.

Everyone will be happy to know that there is another option, but it takes time and work. The thing to remember is that believe it or not, you have at least as much influence on your relationship with your parents as they do, probably even more.

Let's review. When parents have kids, they are directly responsible for their child's welfare throughout both the infancy and childhood stages. Any parent of any newborn will tell you just how much work it is to care for an infant, but they also won't hesitate to tell you how rewarding it is. Quite simply, no infant could survive without the care and attention of a parent. This intense nurturing is necessary throughout childhood, which sort of leaves parents managing their kids' lives. Parents choose your doctor, pick your day care and kindergarten, buy most of your clothes, help you organize your homework, plan vacations for you, and help you choose many of your activities. Everybody wins – you reap the benefit of their support, and they are rewarded with a wonderful kid! If you've forgotten how nice this relationship is, think back to how you felt about your parents when you were seven. Geoff, 16, says:

As a kid I loved to ride with my dad in the car.
I made him beep the horn to all my friends on
the street. I even tried to sit just like him,
with my hand out the window and holding onto

the roof — of course I had to sit on my knees to
do this.

And Claire, 15:

When I was seven I was positive that my mom was
the smartest person in the world. I even said it
to all my friends and teachers.

Your parents also remember your feelings about them, because all
that adoration felt great to them, too! Cheri, 43, remembers this:

When Gerald was a little kid he used to always
want to be with me and help me out with whatever
I was doing. I loved it, it made me feel like
such a good mom. And whenever I asked him how
his day went at school he would talk nonstop for
thirty minutes about all the details of his day.

And Calvin, 43:

I still remember how Kira used to love to crawl
on my lap and up around my shoulders. She loved
to rest her head against mine and tell anybody
who was listening what a great dad I was and how
much she loved me. To remember that makes it
hard to believe that we are the same people
today, eight years later.

When you hit middle school and high school and want to change the
relationship you have with your parents, they get hurt and confused.
Sure, they felt that way about their parents when *they* were your age,
but they're still surprised by your reaction because they feel they're
doing such a better job than their parents did. As a result, parents
typically make one of two classic mistakes: they either fight you for
control of your life or they give up entirely. If they fight you for control, then most of your interactions with them are going to involve a
battle of wills – be it about doing your homework, cleaning your
room, or taking out the trash. This is no fun, but to make matters
worse, you'll often feel compelled to do the exact opposite of what

they suggest, even if you secretly agree with their suggestion. This becomes the only way you can assert your growing independence, as Cynthia, 16, points out:

> One night I was working on this paper in my room. I had been writing for about an hour and was really into it. Then my mom knocked and opened the door at the same time (which I hate) and stuck her head into my room. She said she just wanted to know if I had soccer practice after school. But she stared at the computer monitor the entire time. She was just checking up on me! I was so angry I yelled at her to leave me alone, slammed the door, and called my friend Rachel. I never did finish the paper. Then when my teacher asked why it wasn't done all I could think to say was "It's my mother's fault!" But of course I didn't. I just sort of shrugged it off. I know he'll call my mom and I'll get in trouble when I get home tonight. It's frustrating. If she would just leave me alone things would be fine.

Clearly, shooting yourself in the foot like this is not a useful way of relating to your parents. On the other hand, having them cave in all the time is even more overwhelming, as Donna, 15, realizes:

> My friends think I have it pretty easy. My parents never tell me what to do, in fact, they go along with whatever I suggest. They even let me and my friends party down in the basement — we just have to make sure nobody drives themselves home after partying. But sometimes I wish they would say no or get in my face or something. Sometimes I just need to know where they stand. I have to do everything for myself, and I'm not ready for all that responsibility yet. It's like they would rather be my friends than my parents.

Given all the issues in your life and the decisions you have to make, it's nice to have other opinions and ideas to consider — even from your parents. Ultimately, the decisions are yours, but without some strong ideas and opinions around you how are you ever going to figure out where you stand? The crux of your changing relationship with your parents is that they need to forget about trying to control you anymore, and instead, work more at listening, counseling, and supporting your decision-making muscles. While they don't have control over you anymore, they do have lots of influence, should they choose to use it. But for parents, thinking in terms of influence rather than control is confusing and scary, even if ultimately rewarding. So, you have to teach your parents this, as they're not going to get it on their own. They need to give up acting as your manager, and you need to accept (and encourage!) their new role as consultant and advisor. This transition is never very smooth, even though most parents, like Jesse, 44, understand it in their heads:

```
I'm really trying to give Alex more control over
his life but it's difficult. It's like I have to
relearn how to be a parent when I don't want to.
I really liked the old way, I was good at it. But
I'm not so good at this new relationship. Being
a parent used to be a boost to my self-esteem,
but now it is destroying my self-esteem.
```

Clearly your parents need some help – here are some things you can do:

1. **Be understanding.** For just a minute, put yourself in their place. Think of a relationship or friendship that went bad overnight and then you'll understand what it feels like to them. They're lost and aren't sure of how to respond, especially since they don't feel like they have any choice in the matter.

2. **Acknowledge their confusion.** They're probably way more confused than you are right now, so let them know you understand. Make a brief comment to them or maybe even jot down a short note. Here's an example:

```
Mom and Dad,

I know it's scary being the parent of a teenager
these days. There are lots of terrible things
out there that could happen to me, even when I
```

am being good. And I know it's hard for you with
me not needing you like I did when I was a little
kid. But I have to learn to take care of myself —
not all at once, but probably faster than you
want. Don't give up on me and I won't give up
on you.

Love, Tiana

3. **Give them a role to play.** Telling them just to leave you alone isn't much of a role to play, so give them something more tangible to do that lets them feel like good parents. For instance, ask them not to cross-examine you when you come home from school. Ask for some time by yourself to relax and then tell them to ask about your day *after* dinner. And remind them not to take it personally if you don't always have something to say. Or you might say to them, "Don't ask me a million questions about my homework, but do support me in working hard. Trust that I'll ask for your help when I need it."

4. **Catch them being good.** It's easy to catch people being bad, but it takes a lot more work to catch them being good, especially when these people are your parents. It's also the fastest way to get them to give up trying to manage your life. So, when you see them hold back a comment or question, or give you more responsibility than expected, acknowledge their efforts and give them your appreciation. Nothing too gushy — a simple "thanks" or even just making eye contact with a pat on the back will more than do.

Also, remember that for your parents, it's the little things that count. If you go out of your way for them once in a while, it will usually come back to you many times over, as Reggie, 15, found out:

I used to fight with my parents over the dishes
every night. But then one night it occurred to
me to just go along with them to see how they
reacted. At first they didn't trust what I was
doing. But after a couple of nights they saw I
was just doing it for them (because I could live
with dirty dishes for a long time). It was no big

```
deal to me, but I saw it was a big deal to
them. That felt good, and most importantly they
started to go out of their way for me after
that. As silly as it sounds, that was the begin-
ning of peace in my relationship with them.
```

Give it a try; you'll probably be surprised by the results.

When it comes to parental concern, there's one more big area to discuss: health and safety. These are issues they're going to take a strong stand on, and they should. From a parent's perspective, drinking and driving and having unsafe sex are not negotiable. Granted, it's almost impossible for them to enforce this (short of chaining themselves to you), but they can and should make it really clear where they stand. Letting your parents know that you under-stand this by way of your thoughts and actions will make it much easier for them to grant you freedom in other areas. Says Stanley, 49:

```
Lucy called one night very late. She had been
drinking — strictly against our wishes — and didn't
want to drive home. She asked if I would pick her
up. I almost said no, but then I realized what a
gift this was — she was being responsible about
being irresponsible. What more could a parent
ask for? Sure, the next day she got grounded
for drinking, but not without me telling her
how proud I was of her decision to call me.
I know it sounds crazy, but after this I trust
her a lot more.
```

And Derek, 16:

```
For the last couple of months my dad and I have
been fighting like crazy. I feel like he growls
every time I walk into the room. And whenever he
tells me to do something I absolutely refuse.
Whatever he says, I do the opposite. It isn't
much fun for either of us, but we're both
stubborn so it'll probably take awhile to work
```

through. Anyway, two nights ago I found a
folded-up note under my door:

Jake,
I know we have been at each other these last few
weeks. It doesn't feel too good to me, but right
now I don't know any other way. I expect you
feel pretty much the same. But even though it
doesn't feel this way now, I want you to know
that I love you, and always will. I am very
proud of you too. And yes, we'll probably fight
like cats and dogs for awhile longer, but please
don't ever forget that I love you, no matter how
I act sometimes.
Love, Dad

The note blew me away. I didn't know what to do.
But then a couple of days later I figured it out.
I slipped an old postcard under his door with
two words written on it: "Me too."

Sometimes all it takes to cure a bad situation between you and
your parents is a little show of mutual respect and understanding.
Even if your parents aren't as forward as Derek's dad seems to be,
taking the initiative yourself might prove more rewarding then you
ever thought possible. Give it a try, and don't forget to be patient
with them. They're learning, too.

Irresponsible parents

> Creative minds always have been known
> to survive any kind of bad training.
> Anna Freud

So far I've just been assuming that your parents are doing a reason-
ably good job raising you, or are at least trying their best, but this isn't
always the case. Sometimes parents are neglectful, and at other
times they're even worse than that. Says Lance, 16:

My dad is a very mean and selfish person. I have
no idea why my mom stays with him. He drinks a

lot, and when he does, he yells and threatens us all. My house is a scary place when he has been drinking.

And Shelby, 15:

> My mom just doesn't seem to care all that much. She never asks about school and never shows up for any of my games. I'm not even sure if she knows I am the captain of the soccer team. She isn't mean or anything, she just doesn't pay much attention to me and my brother.

If you have an irresponsible parent, then you've probably had to grow up more quickly than your classmates. Fortunately, you're much more resilient than you think, and there are plenty of other places to turn for support. It's still difficult, though, as Anna, 17, notes:

> I've gotten over getting angry at my dad. He can't even take care of himself, so I don't know how I could expect him to take care of me. Sometimes I feel like his parent more than his daughter, but that's the way it goes. I know I'm missing out on lots of things other teenagers are doing because of this, but I don't see much choice.

And Sandra, 15:

> A couple of the teachers are understanding about what is happening at home. With my parents in the middle of a divorce there just doesn't seem to be any attention left over for me and my needs. One of my teachers, Mr. James, brings me a muffin and juice every Friday morning, just to check in and see how I'm doing with everything.

Although they may disappoint you, the fact is that your parents are probably doing the best they can. If their best is not good enough, then you're going to have to make up the difference for yourself (see the chapter on Other Adults, beginning on page 104, for more info). On the other hand, if their best is more than good enough, be sure to share that support with a friend. Cecil, 16, shows how much that support can mean:

> Jeremy's parents are real nice. They know
> what's happening at my house, so whenever they
> go on a family outing they invite me. Then they
> act like it's no big deal and I'm the one doing
> them the favor by coming along.

THINK ABOUT IT

You're going to do the following twice, once for each of your parents. If one of your parents is dead, or if you don't know one of them, or if you're adopted, use the people who are like parents to you.

1. Find a place where you can sit comfortably and undisturbed for about ten minutes. Take a few deep breaths and let the tension out of your body. Close your eyes if that helps you relax.

2. Imagine yourself sitting in a room – a real or imaginary one. Across from you is an empty chair.

   a. See your parent walk into the room, make eye contact with you, and take the seat directly across from you.

   b. Gaze at your parent's face. Is it relaxed? Tense? Worried? Serene? Really look at the structure and expression.

   c. Tell your parent what you're thinking as you look at their face.

   d. Tell your parent what you're feeling as you look at their face.

   e. Now tell your parent what you want as you look at their face. You might be surprised at what comes up – don't worry, just tell them clearly what you want.

   f. Float your consciousness over to your parent, and through their eyes take a look back at you, their child. From your parent's perspective: What are you thinking? What are you feeling? What do you want?

   g. Float back to your own chair. Now reach out with your hand and gently touch the side of your parent's face. Notice what it feels like.

h. Now make eye contact with your parent again as they get up, nod towards you, and leave the room.

(Go back and do this again for your other parent.)

3. Take a moment to remember that your parents are doing the best job they can – in some cases this isn't too good, but it's the best they can do for a variety of reasons. Most importantly, see that you have at least as much influence over your relationship with them as they do, maybe even more.

4. Slowly stretch and take a few minutes to reflect on what this exercise was like. You might want to take a walk or write for a little bit, but that's up to you.

MORE READING:

Bringing Up Parents: The Teenager's Handbook by Alex J. Packer.
Uncommon Sense For Parents With Teenagers by Michael Riera.

11

divorce

People change and forget to tell each other.

Lillian Hellman

If your family has gone through a divorce, it has certainly affected you in many ways. But no matter what has happened, it's very important to remember that *kids don't cause divorce, bad relationships — not bad people — cause divorce.* Too many kids blame themselves (at least in part) for their parents' divorce, as Alex, 14, did:

> My parents got divorced when I was in seventh
> grade. I got in lots of trouble during school
> then, which stressed them out. I'm not saying
> that's the only reason they got divorced, but
> I'm sure it had something to do with it.

I can almost guarantee that Alex's behavior had nothing to do with his parents' divorce. Sure, all parents feel responsibile for and stressed out about their kids, but none of this causes divorce. In fact, many psychologists believe that kids will unconsciously get themselves into trouble to divert their parents' attention from their relationship, and thus away from their conflicts. Alex may have actually been trying to ensure – the best way he knew how – that his parents stayed together. This may seem strange, but the longer you sit with it the more sense it makes. Try it out.

Again, the reason for your parents' divorce was not you, but their relationship. Either the relationship was never solid or it failed to grow with them. People change, and if their relationship doesn't change with them, it's in trouble. Says Sharon, 45:

```
We were in love when we got married — fifteen
years ago. But we have each changed a great
deal over those years. Now, four careers and two
children later, we don't have much in common. We
definitely care for one another, but we're not in
love with each other, which is why we got
divorced. What keeps us in touch and in communi-
cation with one another is that we both love our
family. That will never change.
```

Having divorced parents is tough to talk about, mainly because there's no easy way to bring it up. Unlike a broken leg, which is obvious to everyone around you, a divorce is invisible unless you choose to reveal it. As a result, there's a tendency for people to keep their thoughts and feelings about the divorce to themselves, which is unfortunate since the best source of support for you comes from your peers, especially those who have also experienced divorce in their family. Jenni, 17, got a lot of help from a guy in her class:

```
At the beginning of senior year, my English
class went on a field trip together. I ended up
sitting next to this guy that I hardly knew. I
was peeved at first; I couldn't imagine sitting
next to this guy for an hour making small talk.
The first five minutes were unbearable, but
then, almost in passing, he mentioned how he had
forgotten his English notebook [for this trip]
at his dad's house over the weekend. He was
annoyed because he wouldn't be able to get it
back until he went back to his dad's house on
Wednesday. This was when I asked how long his
```

parents had been divorced. He talked about the
divorce for a few minutes, and then I told him
how my parents were in the middle of getting a
divorce. (I couldn't believe I was saying this
to him, only my best friend knew anything about
this, and I swore her to secrecy.) The next
thing I knew an hour had passed. He and I still
get together once in a while to talk about the
divorce. What's really weird is that it's easier to talk to him about this than to my best
friend whose parents are still together.

If you take a look at your classmates, at least a third to a half of them have divorced parents. This means that there are plenty of people to talk to and learn from. Opening up to one of them can give you lots of support, as well as an understanding of some of the basic issues of divorce. They'll probably be happy to have someone to share their thoughts with, too.

What divorce feels like

Things are often the worst right when the separation or divorce moves from an abstract idea into reality – when one of your parents moves out, leaving you behind or taking you with them. Prior to the actual move, your parents' conflicts are fairly separate from your daily life, but when one parent moves all this changes. Suddenly things are neither logical nor removed at all! In fact, things can also get kind of ugly at this point, no matter how sane your parents have been up until now. Sasha, 14, went through this:

My parents got divorced when I was in ninth
grade. At first it was strange, they talked to me
and my brother [a senior] about it like it
was no big deal. They had just grown in different ways and it was best for everyone if they
divorced. Yeah, right! But then when my dad
finally moved out a month later it was crazy.
They yelled and screamed at each other, fought
over what furniture my father could take, and

argued about how we would spend time between
their two places. After awhile my brother and I
just left. We ended up getting stoned and going
for a long hike.

When someone moves out the emotional reality of the divorce hits
you square in the face because no matter what has happened between
your parents, you still love them both. This leaves you wondering
how you can remain loyal to each when one or both of them wants
you to show your loyalty by being disloyal to the other. This will drive
you crazy, and you might find yourself saying things you don't even
believe just to avoid feeling disloyal to one of them. Says Sherri, 16:

Whenever I'm with my dad he'll take at least one
cheap shot at my mom. "So, is your mom still
just working part-time at the clothing store?"
Now, even though I agree with him that she
should get a better job or at least work full-
time, there's no way I can tell him this. So I
end up defending my mom and justifying her work,
even though I don't believe what I'm saying.

Or Claire, 15:

Whenever my mom makes fun of my dad's new girlfriend I'm careful to stay neutral. If I agree
with her I feel guilty. Usually I just try and
change the subject, but if she really sticks
with it I'll end up defending my dad, even
though much of the time I agree with my mom.

There's no easy solution to any of this. A child-psychologist friend of
mine offers the following story:

I was working with a 4-year-old boy whose parents had just divorced. We were doing play
therapy together. The boy loved to play army
wars in the sandbox. Each week he would come
in and assemble the armies on either side of a
line he drew in the sand. Then the battle would

commence. The armies were fighting over a jewel
that the victor kept for the week between bat-
tles. And whichever army won one week, lost the
following week. After a couple of months of this
I asked the boy what it was like to be the jewel
that his parents were fighting over. The boy
welled up with tears and hugged me.

Everyone has a hard time balancing their loyalty between both parents, no matter what the circumstances of the divorce are. So, when
you feel like you're going a little crazy, realize that you aren't, and
that all people in your shoes have this dilema. Recognize that you're
being asked to stay sane in a crazy situation, and surely at some point
you're bound to feel a little crazed yourself!

Custody arrangements

This part of the divorce most directly affects you and your life, as an
agreement must be reached about where you will stay. How much say
you want to have in this decision is up to you, but because of the loyalty issues we just discussed most kids don't want much to do with it
at all. Rasheed, 15, agrees:

There was no way I was going to decide who I
would spend the most time with. That's their
job. The only thing I made clear is that I didn't
want to be shuffled back and forth like a hockey
puck. It's a real pain going back and forth
between two places.

Or Stevie, 16, offers this:

The only thing I cared about was that I could
stay in the same school. I didn't want to have to
go to one school one year and then another school
another year. One of my friends had to do that
all through high school and it drove him nuts.

If you *do* have a preference or opinion, and feel comfortable stating
it, then by all means do! It might make a big difference in the way you
feel about the whole divorce.

One note of caution: Like everything else in a family there are two agreements, the stated one and the actual one. This means that although your parents have reached a custody agreement, they may not always adhere to it. Expect the arrangements to change from time to time, and don't be surprised if you're not included in the discussion. If you find this happening, gently remind them that shared custody is an inconvenience for everybody, and that inconvenience needs to be shared by all. In other words, just because you're a teenager doesn't mean you should bear all the burden. Ilana, 15, knows what this can be like:

```
My parents are so selfish sometimes. Like my
mom (or dad) will call me at school and leave
a message for me to go to my dad's house instead
of hers after school that day. What about me?
It seems like they never consider my plans. You
know, maybe I needed to go to her house instead
of my dad's for one reason or another. Or what if
I never got the message? It sucks. I can't wait
until I get my license so I don't have to depend
on them for rides. I'm already saving my money
to buy a car.
```

A divorce, like any other tragedy, forces you to grow up quickly in order to cope. This rush to grow up is painful and takes time; it's as if somebody came up to you one day and said that you had to run a marathon a month from now. You could do it, but you'd probably not be doing very much other than training. Well, the same is true for learning to cope with divorce. Many experts feel that it takes one full year from when the actual papers are signed (not when the separation begins) for kids to regain their balance, and of course this assumes that everything was in balance before the divorce. Take heart, though, because the cliché is true: This *will* make you a stronger person in the long run.

Parents' lovers

If your parents are divorced then there's a good chance that one or both of them will get involved in other relationships in the future.

This means you're going to have to get used to seeing your parents with other people. You don't have to like it, but you do have to adjust to it, as Katherine, 16, did:

> It was hard just getting used to the divorce, but my parents dating other people is just plain bizarre. Sometimes I feel more like their friend — advising them on what to wear or where to go on a date — than their 16-year-old daughter. I'm dreading the day when I wake up and one of these dates has turned into an over-nighter. They both swear that it'll never happen without talking to me first, but then they promised they'd never get divorced either.

And Ricky, 16:

> My mother has been seeing this guy, Alexander, for a while now. I guess he's okay, but I can tell he doesn't know what to do with me. Should he treat me like a kid, a son, a friend, or what? I know it's real important to him that I like him (because it's important to my mom that I like him). And I do like him, but there's no way I could ever like him more than my dad. I know, I know, he's not trying to take my dad's place. I really do understand this. But then how come I feel so guilty when I have a good time with him and my mom? It gets complicated real fast — I never realized how easy I had it when they were together.

Remember, your responsibility is not to like or even enjoy this new person in your parent's life, only to treat them civilly. In most cases, it's not their fault that your parents are divorced, even if it might appear that way. Stephanie, 45, says of her divorce:

> I know it's difficult to accept, but the reason we got divorced isn't because of the affair I had. The affair just made me realize how far

things had slipped between Laurence and me. I
know Suzanne [her 16-year-old daughter] doesn't
understand or believe this, but it is the truth —
at least from my perspective.

In any case, new people will enter your parents' — and your — life. Be patient, because finding a relationship that's comfortable with this new person takes time and there will probably be a testing period that will have to pass before you will take their presence seriously. Says Lewis, 16:

The first time my mom introduced me to a boyfriend of hers I was real nice to him. I talked
a lot and asked him lots of questions about himself. I really went out of my way. Well, that
was three years and five boyfriends ago. Now I
won't even take the guy seriously unless he has
been around for a few months and really tries
to reach out to me. I'm pretty tough to get to
these days.

Remarriage

Having one of your parents remarry is a *really* big deal, especially if you live with that parent on a semi-regular basis. It gets even more confusing if their new spouse has kids, too. Says Sheila, 17:

When my mom and George decided to get remarried
it got complicated real fast. George has two
little kids who spend every other week with him,
and since I spend half of each week with my dad
and half with my mom, the scheduling was a
nightmare. What's worse is that I don't like
George's kids at all — I can barely tolerate him.
    Then they had to decide whose house to live
in, which was real hard because they don't even
live in the same town — and there was no way I was
changing schools for him! In the end we moved
into his house. It really sucked having to move
all my stuff into this tiny room at the back of

his house. I feel like an afterthought. And in return for moving they bought me my own car so I can stay in the same high school, even though I have to drive forty minutes to school every-day. The car is cool and all, but it isn't worth it. Well, actually, the car is more like my home now than either my dad's or my mom's house.

On the other hand, if the new spouse moves in with you that also gets confusing quickly, as Diana, 16, points out:

When Sam moved in with us it was strange. I'm not used to anybody in our house except my mom and me. Then he began to move things around, which really bothered me. After a couple of weeks I couldn't find anything in the kitchen anymore and all these strange foods started showing up in the refrigerator. I like my routines. It took us about a year to get used to living under the same roof, but I still don't like it.

Physical space aside, the new marriage also complicates your life emotionally. Probably the first question you're going to have to deal with is what kind of role this new person is going to play in your life. Kit, 15, says:

Right away I could tell she was going to try and take the place of my mom. She wanted to make me lunch, give me rides to school, and check on my homework. There was no way. After a bunch of screaming matches she finally backed off. I can deal with her and my father loving one another, but I'm not looking for another mother. I already have one and that's enough for me.

And Olinda, 16:

The day after we moved into Kathy's house [after they got married] she took me out for a long walk. She knew it was hard for me. She told me that all she wanted was to be friends — she didn't think it was her role to try and parent me. She hoped that eventually I would come to like and trust her, but that it wasn't necessary for us to live peacefully together. Then she gave me lots of space in that first six months, which helped.

Remarriage is tricky for everybody involved, including the other parent, as Helen, 15, found out;

After my mom got remarried to Cecil, my dad would ask me a million questions every time I was staying at his house. He wanted to know all sorts of crazy things: what they ate, how often they spoke on the phone, when they went to bed, and how Cecil was treating me. He was especially interested in what I thought of Cecil. I had to be careful about this, because while I liked Cecil I didn't want to give my dad the impression that Cecil was taking his place, which is what I think he was afraid of. It was awful seeing my dad so vulnerable.

And that vulnerability is real, as remarriage is the final piece of the divorce. Once one of your parents remarries, there is no chance of them getting back together with your other parent, which is a fantasy that most people cling to as long as possible, as Veronica, 15, did:

Even though I like Cheryl, I had a tough time with her and my dad getting married. My brother and I were still secretly hoping that my dad and mom would get back together again. Recently they seemed to be getting along again. But I guess this marriage kills those hopes.

Finally, remember that divorce (and all that follows) is difficult on everybody. Nobody in the family is unaffected. The most difficult part for you is that you're forced to remain passive, because the decision to divorce is up to your parents. However, once this decision is made, it's vitally important to once again get active on your own behalf. Let your feelings be known and insist on input into the decisions that affect you directly. If you do this, you will not only have more say in your life, but you'll also have a bigger perspective on things, like Marisha, 17, did:

> I was pissed when my parents told me they were getting divorced, and I told them so. Then I made sure to stick up for myself along the way — made sure I didn't have to change schools, made sure custody arrangements worked for me, too, and refused to listen to either of them gossip about the other one. Then, six months ago, my dad told me he was getting remarried. I'm not real happy about it (I don't like the woman that much) but I have to admit that he's real happy with her, which is good to see. In fact, he's happier than I can remember. So I guess I'm happy for him, which really surprises me considering how I felt when Mom and Dad told me they were getting divorced.

THINK ABOUT IT

While the emotions around divorce are difficult, the day-to-day inconveniences are often just as troublesome because you have little control over them. This will help you appreciate all the changes a divorce causes.

1. If your parents were to get divorced and share custody of you, how would that affect your day-to-day life? Think of as many things as you can, including transportation, your bedroom(s), meals, phone calls, clothes storage, holidays, birthday reminders, money, driver's licence, and homework.

2. How would this change if one of your parents fell in love and got remarried?

MORE READING:

Maya's Divided World by Gloria Velasquez.

12

other adults

The impossible is often the untried.
Jim Goodwin

You should realize that there are lots of adults other than your parents that you can turn to for support. This includes the teachers, coaches, neighbors, and clergy in your life who have a different relationship with you than your parents do. These relationships will change even more between your freshman and senior years; as a freshman you may wonder how your math teacher could be an important and supportive person in your life, but as Rachel, 17, found out, it does happen:

As a ninth-grader I felt that all adults thought like my parents and were all pretty much alike. They had the authority and we the students did not. But as I got older I realized that some (not all) of my teachers don't fit that stereotype — some of them are okay, more than okay in fact. I can talk with my English teacher about things I don't tell my friends or family. It's not that she's my friend, it's more that she's an adult

I can trust. I know that after I graduate we'll stay in touch, maybe even become friends a few years down the road.

Sure, there are adults that cling to their authority as teachers and coaches, but there are many who don't. These people aren't exactly friends, but they aren't authority figures either. Says Crystal, 18:

I don't know how I would have made it through high school without Mr. Leider. He helped me through all sorts of things: a disastrous love affair, an anorexic friend, and screaming parents. He never told me what to do, either; mostly he just listened and took me seriously, which is what I needed most. And I knew that I could trust him not to tell anyone what I talked to him about. It isn't that we talked all the time — probably only once or twice a semester — but when we did it was helpful and lasted a long time.

And Shawna, 17:

My volleyball coach was a great ally during high school. She knew how to push me when I was just about to give up on myself. And even though she listened when I needed to talk about my problems, she never cut me any slack because of them either. She was both supportive and fair. I'm really thankful she was there for me.

This change – from seeing all adults as authority figures to seeing some of them as allies – is a gradual shift over the course of your time in high school. It's natural, and, in fact, important, to find an adult ally in high school. Ironically, non-parent adults often have a clearer perspective of you than your own parents do, as they aren't as attached. (If you don't believe this, try talking to the teenage kids of some of your favorite adults.) They have less at stake in your development and much less history with you. While you can be a young adult in *their* eyes, it's difficult not to be a child in your parents'. Elizabeth, 15, says:

> It's strange, when Ms. Seeney looks at me I know
> she sees me as responsible and mature for my
> age. But when my parents look at me I know they
> see a little kid who doesn't clean up after her-
> self, doesn't do her homework without lots of
> nagging, and talks on the phone all night. I wish
> my parents would see me like Ms. Sweeney does.

These adults are also extremely helpful when you have those to-be-expected high school problems. Beverly, 40, says:

> I've been teaching for twenty years now and
> some of my most rewarding moments have come
> when talking to students one-on-one about their
> lives. I don't know enough to tell them how to
> solve their problems, but I know enough not to
> tell them what to do. After a little fumbling
> in the dark they usually turn out just fine.
> Though there have been a few times when I really
> encouraged them to see a professional counselor,
> as what was bothering them was way beyond me —
> things like eating disorders, deep depression,
> and other more serious problems.

Beverly touches on an important point – there are certain problems that require professional assistance that a teacher or coach may not be able to help you with. In these cases, seriously consider seeking the assistance they suggest. It's not only better for you, but also better for your relationship with that adult because if you don't get the appropriate assistance, your teacher or coach often ends up feeling responsible for your well-being, which will make them more like a parent than you might want.

Another really important thing that you need to be aware of is that if you have been the victim of some sort of physical or sexual abuse in your family, and if you tell a teacher or coach about it, they are re-quired, by law, to report the abuse to the appropriate state agency –

usually within 24 hours. All teenagers (and families) need to understand that they have no choice in this matter. Abuse like this is so
unfair to kids that states have wisely chosen to require educators to
report the offense. Laura, 15, experienced this:

> When I was a sophomore I told a teacher about
> my stepfather forcing himself on me when nobody
> was at home. It was so awful I just had to tell
> somebody, only I didn't realize that she had to
> report it to Child Protective Services. When she
> told me this I got real angry at her, called her
> all sorts of names, and walked out on her. To her
> credit she tracked me down later in the day to
> talk. She again told me she had to report it but
> she wanted to talk with me before doing so. She
> really wanted me to understand what was happen-
> ing. I was scared, but I listened to what she had
> to say. In the end I sat in the room with her
> while she made the call — I even got on the phone
> myself. My teacher and the person on the phone
> made me see how wrong it was [what my stepdad
> was doing to me]. He ended up getting in some
> trouble, but mostly he just had to go to coun-
> seling. But the best part was that he saw that
> he couldn't mess with me anymore.

On the other side of the coin, Don, 34, says:

> A couple of years ago a student was in my room
> seeking some extra help when I noticed a bruise
> on the side of her face. When I asked her what
> happened she said, rather unconvincingly, that
> she had slipped off the stairs and hit her head
> against the wall. I must have looked like I
> didn't believe her, because seconds later she
> was in tears. I asked what was wrong a few times,
> and then she finally blurted out that her father
> had hit her in the face the night before — he had
> been drinking. We talked for a long while about

```
it. Then I told her what I dreaded saying: "You
know, legally I have to report this." I watched
the blood drain out of her face as she
understood what I was saying. We talked a while
longer. In the end I promised not to call until
the next day, after we had talked again. By then
she seemed to understand it was for the best,
and we made the call together. Making that call
was hard for me, I'm only glad the law didn't
give me any choice. I'm fearful that if I had
had the choice I would not have made the call.
And the way things turned out, it was an
important step to take.
```

If you find yourself in this situation, try to understand the position your adult confidant is in, and try to remember that the law is designed to protect you even if it's scary to imagine enacting it.

By the time you graduate you'll probably have had some good talks with at least some of your teachers; take advantage of the support the ones you trust are offering and steer clear of the others. These teachers also help you see how adults other than your parents lead their lives, giving you a broader perspective.

THINK ABOUT IT

The idea here isn't to get you to talk to adults differently than you already do, but to recognize your potential to relate to some adults differently.

1. Name two adults (not your parents) that you like.
   a.

   b.

2. Think about your relationship with each of them, making sure to consider the *relationship*, not the actual person. Describe how you communicate, what your level of trust is, and the types of conversations you have.

a.

b.

3. Think of two things in your life that are currently bothering you —
   minor annoyances or major problems. Now imagine talking to
   each of the adults about these two problems. How does it feel? Is
   one problem easier to talk about than the other? Do you feel more
   comfortable with one person or the other? Do you trust this person enough to tell them everything that's happening? How do
   they respond to what you have to say? Are they helpful? Describe
   what these conversations would be like.
   a.

   b.

13

Those who do not know how to weep
with their whole heart don't know how
to laugh either.

Golda Meir

By now you know that death is a difficult, yet natural and unavoidable, part of life. Some of you may have experienced the death of somebody close to you – a family member, personal friend, friend of the family, or neighbor. Or if not, it's possible that a close friend of yours will have gone through such an experience. For the purposes of this book, we're going to focus on the death of a loved one, since this is the greatest loss a person can face. But what's described here is true for any kind of grief and loss, whether or not it involves death. To continue, depending on how close you were to the deceased, the death can dramatically alter the quality and direction of your life. Says Tristan, 15:

> When my mom died it was like my lifeline to
> the planet was cut. I drifted for a long time.
> Friends and family noticed, but they couldn't do
> anything to help me. They even tried putting me
> in therapy. But nothing helped because I wasn't

ready to come back. I had to do it on my own in
my own time.

And Tony, 16:

I was basically out of control after my brother
died. Everything was so superficial compared to
his dying. Nothing was worth anything to me so
I got reckless. I tried anything and everything.
I think I secretly hoped that I would have an
accident and die.

And Khris, 20:

After my dad died I just buried my head in my
books. I worked and studied harder than ever
before — I wanted to do well for my father.
Nothing else mattered to me. Most of my friends
gave up on me. It's only now [sophomore year in
college] that I realize how depressed I was. I
kept the pain and depression hidden from myself
by working so hard, but now I have to face the
pain and confusion. There's no escaping it.

How people grieve is, like everything else, a personal and individual
matter; what works for one person is not the answer for another.
However, there are certain responses that everybody goes through
when they lose someone special. While these responses are presented in a specific order here, please realize that going through
these feelings isn't anywhere near as ordered. The reality is much
more random, a more circular progression rather than a step-by-step
one. The figure below shows what that cycle looks like, and following
that, there is a brief description of each stage.

The grief cycle

- **Denial and Isolation:** In this period you try to act like the death
  never happened, or that the loss doesn't hurt that much. You
  might also prefer to be alone at this point or away from people
  who will discuss the death with you. Blair, 15, tells what it's like:

When friends told me how sorry they were to hear
that my father died I usually just shrugged it
off and said things like: "Yeah, thanks, but
things will be okay. We'll survive." For the most
part I just wasn't feeling anything — I was numb.

And Isaac, 16:

When my mom died I didn't like being around all
my relatives. It was too much for me to handle,
so I usually just stayed up in my room or went
out for a ride. It was like, "Yeah, she's dead.
So get out of my face and let me deal with it in
my own way." I know they were trying to be helpful by getting me to talk, but honestly, that
was the last thing I needed.

- **Anger:** In this period almost anything can provoke an outburst from you. You're also likely to be angry at life in general, as well as at just about every adult or friend who hasn't kept their word with you. Says Sara, 17:

A few months after her death [Sara's sister] I
started to get angry at everything and everybody

```
around me. This was strange, because I hardly
ever lose my temper. But at that time I was con-
stantly on the verge of ramming any car that
cut me off or didn't signal a turn. If my little
brother even looked at me the wrong way I was
all over him — verbally and physically. It was
all very strange. I wasn't myself at all, which
was scary.
```

Although it might be completely out of character, another thing you might find yourself doing is getting envious of friends who haven't suffered a similar loss. You may even resent them for not appreciating what they have, as Barry, 15, did:

```
I really hate it when my friends bitch about
their parents being too strict or whatever.
I would love to be able to still argue with my
father. People just don't appreciate what they
have until it's too late.
```

- **Bargaining:** This is when you try to make your behavior change the outcome of the situation. It's most common when you're dealing with the terminal illness of someone close to you, hoping that you can reverse the problem by way of your actions. Allison, 14, describes what that's like:

```
When my grandmother was dying I remember making
a bunch of different deals with God. Things
like, "I will be nice to everybody and you will
make my grandma better" and "I will be respon-
sible around home and take care of my little
sister and you will make my grandma better."
Deep down I think I knew that it wouldn't make a
difference. But at least it helped me feel like
I was doing something.
```

- **Depression:** This is when you really begin to feel the loss — when you really deal with the fact that this person is gone from your life.

This period can be completely overwhelming, which is why it's good that we naturally cycle through *all* these phases rather than staying in any one too long. Remaining in the depressed phase would be too much to handle all at once, as life loses its color and often seems not worth living, as Rikki, 16, found out:

```
One morning it really hit me — my father was
dead. I would never ever be able to talk to him
again. It was so sad it took my breath away. I
don't even remember crying, but I do remember
feeling how wet my face was with tears. After
that, nothing seemed worthwhile. Life wasn't
fair and I didn't care. I blew off all my respon-
sibilities and slept or watched television all
the time.
```

• **Acceptance:** At this point you begin to integrate the fact that you've lost someone with your daily life and personal aspirations. The loss itself begins to shrink from being the main focus of your life. The sadness never goes away completely, but, fortunately, the passion and curiosity for life do come back as you reconcile with your grief. Says Grace, 16:

```
It took awhile, but gradually I became more
interested in hanging out with my friends and
doing well in school again. The only constant
throughout was my music. If I hadn't kept play-
ing the piano I'm not sure I would have made it.
Now I'm back to the way I was before my mom
died, only — and I know this sounds corny — I
feel a lot older and wiser. There is more to me
somehow.
```

You can probably look at the figure on page 112 and understand it intellectually, but the reality of living through it is a whole other issue. Although painful and difficult, the pattern is entirely natural, and in fact, you'll probably go through it in some form or another when suffering from other loses like the end of a relationship, having a best friend move away, or failing to reach a goal. Mickey, 17, experienced this when he broke up with Shelly:

When Shelly broke up with me I was just numb. I
couldn't believe it. It took a couple of days
before it sank in. Then I got real angry. "How
could she do this to me? I was the best thing
that ever happened to her. What about all
those promises she made?" After that I tried to
change. I called and told her that I would be
better about calling her and doing things with
her friends. I even said I would spend less time
with my friends. But she wouldn't budge. Finally
I just got real depressed. My mom says I just
moped around the house like a sad puppy for
weeks. But now [a few months later] everything
is fine again.

If for some reason you find yourself getting stuck in one of these
phases then it's probably time to talk to a counselor or doctor (but
chances are, you'll do just fine by yourself). Most people work
through their grief in a natural and healthy way – it's not easy, but
you'll get through it and will probably become a stronger and deeper
person along the way. The one *and only* pay-off for all that pain is
that it gives you depth of character.

THINK ABOUT IT

In trying to come to grips with the death of a loved one, people often
speak of "letting go" and "moving on." Think of a person you've
lost. When that person was alive you had a relationship with them
that was important and vital to you (even if it was someone you didn't
see often). Their death makes it feel like the relationship has died
along with the person, even though the relationship need not die. To
"get on with your life" and "let go of your grief" you need to first
form another relationship with that person. This person was too important to simply forget, and many people will not or cannot "move
on" until they are sure that they will not forget. You need a new relationship that brings that person into yourself; you create a small
space within yourself for them, a place that you can visit whenever
you wish.

You knew this person who died quite well, well enough to know how they would respond to certain situations and certain questions. You knew how they acted and felt when you misbehaved. You knew how to please them. You also knew how to tease them, make them laugh, and anger them. There are many general and idiosyncratic things that you knew about them, and many more things that perhaps you don't yet remember. The idea is to develop an active and flexible memory of them in the present versus a passive and rigid memory of them in the past.

With this in mind, take some time to reflect on the following questions. You will also probably come up with some of your own questions that can help you create a living memory of this person; do whatever helps you keep them alive within you, and you alive within them.

What are some of your favorite mental snapshots of this person? What do you imagine are some of their favorite mental snapshots of you? How about of the two of you together?

When did they surprise you with something they said or did? How did this increase your understanding and appreciation of them? And, how did you surprise them with something you said or did? What did this tell them about you that they didn't know before?

Is there any particular song, book, poem, or art piece that you associate with them? If not, think of one now. What does that represent?

What did this person see in you that was special? How did they communicate this to you? And how did you let them know that you got it?

MORE READING:

On Death And Dying by Elisabeth Kubler-Ross.
The Kids' Book About Death and Dying: By and For Kids by Eric
        F. Rofes and The Unit at Fayerweather Street School.
Straight Talk About Death for Teenagers by Earl A. Grollman.
How It Feels When A Parent Dies by Jill Krementz.

14

personal safety

The man who strikes first admits
that his ideas have given out.
Chinese Proverb

It's unfortunate, but we have to accept that the world isn't always a
safe place. For this reason, it's important that you learn to take care
of yourself. Violent crime is on the rise, which means you need to
learn to take care of yourself at a younger age and in a different way
than your parents did. Of course, where you live has a lot to do with
how you take care of yourself – generally, it's more dangerous in ur-
ban than non-urban areas – but all places have their dangers. We're
going to deal here with the most essential aspects of personal safety:
recognition, intuition, and, as a last resort, self-defense. You need to
know how to spot dangerous situations before they develop, know
what to do or say if they occur, and know how to defend yourself
should the need arise.

Recognition

In Carlos Castenada's writing about his adventure with the Indian
shaman Don Juan he asks Don Juan what he would do if, upon exiting
a building, he realized that there was a man across the street, hidden

in a building, pointing a gun at him, and he responded: "Easy, I would not be there." No matter how much Carlos persisted, Don Juan's response was the same: he would not be there. Well, this is actually the best defense possible – recognizing dangerous situations before they develop and then avoiding them entirely. You don't have to be Don Juan to practice this strategy, as April, 16, realized:

> When I came out of the movies I headed toward the
> shortcut through the alley like I usually do.
> Only this was at night, and for the first time
> I noticed how dark the alley was. Rather than be
> stupid I got in with the crowd and walked around
> the block like everybody else.

There are certainly some unavoidable situations out there, that either happen too quickly or, for one reason or another, you just don't notice. However, if you try to get in the habit of assessing the situation around you at different times, you'll surprise yourself at how much you notice and how many hazardous situations are actually avoidable.

Intuition

If for some reason you fail to see the situation developing, let your intuition tell you what's going on, as it will recognize the situation for what it is long before you do. Furthermore, your intuition will be able to tell you exactly what to do if you learn to pay attention to it and trust it. Andre Salvage, in his defense workshops, says: "Everyone has that voice of intuition and your intuition is never wrong." In fact, when you really start to trust your intuition you'll also get better at recognizing potentially dangerous situations before they develop, as Debbie, 17, found out:

> Something felt really weird about the guy, so
> when he asked for a ride I said no, which isn't
> like me at all. Usually I'm willing to trust peo-
> ple, but there was something about this guy . . .
> it was like this voice was screaming in my head,
> "No! Get rid of this guy! Don't give him a ride!"

If ever you talk to somebody who was attacked, they usually say that they could tell that something was wrong before the assault actually happened. Unfortunately, they didn't listen to their intuition until it was too late, as Jerry, 15, did:

```
Just the way he walked towards me caught my eye.
But like an idiot I dismissed it. In fact I got
angry with myself for watching too many
detective movies. I was wrong. The guy stepped
in front of me and demanded my wallet, and when
I hesitated he whacked me across the side of the
head with a stick he had in his hand. He took my
wallet and left me lying on the sidewalk bleed-
ing and suffering from a concussion.
```

Even if you fail to heed the advice of your intuition as the situation develops, it's still not too late for it to help you, only now you have to listen harder and trust more. One of the main things attackers depend on is confusion, because if they can get you confused they're usually home free. If you can tune into your intuition while things are happening, it will tell you exactly what to do or say. The only catch is that there's no time to second guess what it tells you; when you hear that voice of intuition, you have to act immediately. If you start thinking it over, the confusion comes back to argue. (Besides, there's usually no time to spare.) Attackers count on the fact that most people don't trust their intuition enough to act on it, and so, remain confused, as Abbe, 16, was:

```
Everything happened so fast. I didn't have time
to think. At first this person was asking for
money for a bus ticket and then it was that his
car was broken and his kids were in it and then
he was asking for a ride to his car. All his
stories were mixed-up, and he kept getting in
front of me, steering me towards a broken street
light. It felt all wrong, but instead of walking
away I tried to get his story straight in my
head. But whenever I would ask about the story
```

he would compliment me on how nice I seemed or
how generous I was. Next thing I knew there were
two more people and we were all off in the corner
of the parking lot. Luckily all they wanted was
my money. It could have been much worse.

Besides using confusion, attackers also look to disarm your intuition
by making you angry, embarrassed, or self-conscious. Once you've
lost your calm (and your access to your intuition) you're an easy
mark. Not many people are willing to make a scene in order to protect themselves, no matter how insistent their intuition is, but Darla,
18, proves that it's worth the effort:

I could feel this guy getting too close to me in
line. At first I just moved my purse to the side
and took a step closer to the person in front of
me. But then he matched my step and moved to the
side of my purse. When he did this a couple of
more times I finally turned and in a loud voice
said: "Will you please move away from me and
give me some space before I have to call a
Security Guard!" Then he pretended like he was
innocent and that it was no big deal, but I knew
better. What's a little embarrassment compared
to my safety?

By now you might be thinking: "Yeah, OK, this sounds great and all,
but with all the other voices in my head, how do I know which one is
my intuition?" Great question! First, everyone is familiar with their
intuition, whether they recognize it or not. It's your intuition that lets
you know when someone is flirting with you; it's the same voice that
makes you comfortable or uncomfortable when meeting someone
for the first time; it's the voice that guides you in any spontaneous
performance, like improvising during a saxophone solo or cutting
back across field on a kick-off return. And, as Walker, 17, now realizes, it's the voice that keeps on talking, even if you don't listen to it:

After I had been knocked down this voice kept on
telling me to stay down. And each time I got
back up — and knocked back down — it would say to

stay down. Some part of me knew it was the right
thing to do; too bad I didn't listen.

Self-defense

Unfortunately, violent things happen, so the smart thing to do is to
learn some of the basics of self-defense. This is not to say that everyone should go out and become a martial arts expert, but it does make
sense to take advantage of a weekend workshop on self-defense in
your community. (For resources, check the Yellow Pages under "Self
Defense Instruction," or contact your local YMCA or YWCA.) Most
of these programs teach aspects of recognition and intuition, as well
as actual physical self-defense. A workshop will not only teach you
some techniques to defend yourself, but will also help you develop
the attitude necessary for actually using these techniques. Just learning what to do isn't really enough, as Billie, 15, points out:

> Some of the things they taught us were really
> scary, like sticking your finger into someone's
> eye socket and popping their eye out. There is
> no way I could do that.

Seth, 16, also learned the attitude it takes to follow through:

> One thing they showed us was how to break
> someone's knee by kicking them — it only takes
> 15-20 pounds of force if you kick them in the
> right place. The woman teaching the class must
> have seen a disgusted look on my face because
> she then looked right at me and talked about un-
> derstanding that if someone is attacking you
> they are not a nice person and they deserve
> whatever they get. This includes a busted leg
> for life. When she said this it really clicked
> for me — it's either me or the attacker in a sit-
> uation like this.

You'll not only learn the moves, but also get some experience defending yourself from attackers, both verbally and physically. This
physical experience is particularly essential – since the only other

time it comes up is in a real attack — and both help build confidence. Says Susan, 16:

```
After the workshop I felt more confident about
myself and my ability to take care of myself.
I learned how to stay relaxed and trust myself
when things get frightening or confusing. It
feels great. I hope I never have to actually
defend myself, but if I have to I know that I
can and will.
```

Take advantage of what your community offers and learn to recognize potential dangers and listen to your intuition. A little preparation can go a long way toward keeping you safe.

THINK ABOUT IT

This should help you become more familiar with your voice of intuition.

1. Describe a couple of times in your life when you listened to your voice of intuition.

   a.

   b.

2. Go back to each description and let yourself relive the experience of hearing and feeling your intuition.

3. Write a description of how you recognize your intuition and of how it presents itself to you.

OTHER RESOURCES:

I recommend the personal safety programs designed by Andre Salvage, the Director of Salvage Defense Programs. For more information, contact Andre at (415) 753-2796, or visit him on the World Wide Web at: http://www.Andre-sdp.com. Many of the ideas here have their origins in Andre's work.

15

The time to relax is when you
don't have time for it.
Sydney J. Harris

Stress is a reaction to all the physical, emotional, social, academic, and family changes you're going through – probably something you're very familiar with. Stress isn't necessarily bad, as without some stress not much would get done. Stress is not measured by how involved or active you are, what counts is how you handle your various responsibilities. Theoretically, you could have nine major responsibilities and stay fairly relaxed and at ease (although it's probably unlikely). You could also have only one minor responsibility and be completely stressed out about it (equally improbable). So the key to understanding the stress you feel is to look at how you handle things. There are three major questions to answer:

1. Are your expectations of yourself and others realistic?
2. Are you doing the things that are important to you?
3. Do you learn from your mistakes?

If you can answer yes to these questions then you're probably a balanced and relaxed person. If you're like the rest of us and are still struggling, read on!

Everyone is familiar with the feeling of being "stressed," yet no two people experience it in exactly the same way. Here are a host of responses:

When I get stressed I immediately turn to food, preferably chocolate or ice cream. I can't stop myself, and while I'm eating I feel better. Quincy, 15

When I get stressed I can't eat at all. Just the thought of food makes me nauseous. What really helps me is a cup of coffee and a cigarette with a friend. Phil, 16

Almost every Friday night me and couple of buddies split a case of beer to just get away from the stress of a week at school. We just kick back, have fun, and forget about everything else. Stanley, 17

When I get too stressed I get real horny. If I'm going out with someone it's not a problem, but if I'm not, well, I usually just masturbate. I'm definitely more relaxed afterwards! Josh, 16

When things get too much for me I go for a long hike. The exercise and the clean air calm me down. Helena, 15

Obviously this is just the tip of the iceberg, and there are a million different responses to stress. What's interesting about the variation is that what causes stress for one person is an outlet for another. Each of you is different. Another important point to remember is that, in moderation, none of these behaviors is bad, but in the extreme, even healthy behaviors become problematic. Addictions, eating disorders, and a variety of other problems probably all started as escapes from stress, so watch yourself. Since stress is the natural product of being out of balance, I find it easier and more rewarding to work on getting back *in* balance. Tara, 17, explains:

When I get stressed it's usually because I have lost touch with some part of me. So to get back

```
in balance I have to figure out what is missing
and go out and do it. It could involve exercise,
time alone, working on my drawing, or spending
time with friends. I just know that if I can stay
in touch with these different parts of me then I
can handle a lot more in my day-to-day life.
```

Ironically, it's actually more interesting to *deal* with stress than to get rid of it. Sure, stress is a form of pressure, but pressure is frequently necessary to grow and expand. Yes, too much is overwhelming, but not having enough stress equals boredom. (Don't believe me? Try remembering how you spent your summer days at home in eighth grade. . . .)

Sometimes, events in your life push you way beyond this "healthy" level of stress. Traumatic or other difficult life events not only add stress, *but also affect how much stress you can handle*. Very few people understand this concept. These events build up and become "sedimented stress." When combined with the continually shifting stress of everyday life, sedimented stress really changes your ability to stay in balance.

Stress Buffer Zone

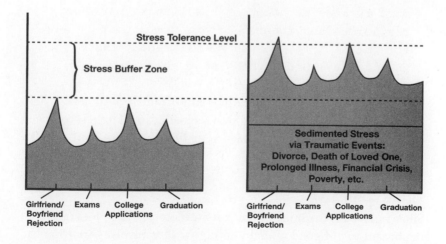

Again, it's critical to recognize how the amount of sedimented stress in a person's life affects how much day-to-day stress they can handle. For a person with just a little sedimented stress, the normal events of high school – exams, college applications, break ups, holidays, and graduation – are all quite manageable. For the person with a great deal of sedimented stress, then these same events are likely to push them past a tolerable level. Says Shelby, 17:

> I really hate most holidays. They are such
> painful reminders of my parents' divorce five
> years ago. To this day we all get in fights
> during the holidays, usually over stupid things.
> I can't wait until I'm old enough to not have
> to come home for the holidays. And, of course,
> my schoolwork falls apart like clockwork every
> year between Thanksgiving and New Year's.

The good news is that, with time, it *is possible* to reduce the amount of sedimented stress in one's life. You do this by talking about and examining these events from a variety of perspectives, which is what good friends, and when appropriate, good counseling, can do.

> My older brother died when I was just five years
> old. I just remember it as an awful time in our
> house. The anniversary of his death is still
> very sad, but in a strange way it has become
> more of a celebration of his life rather than
> the depressing funeral of his death that it was
> for the first few years. We talk about him a lot
> as a family, and I think that helps too.

Again, I cannot overemphasize how important it is to accept help from your friends and family, and to seek additional help if you need it. Remember, the more balanced your life, the more stuff you can handle without undue strain.

THINK ABOUT IT

Since balance is the most important antidote you have for stress, it's important to get good at maintaining it. This involves spotting the first signs of stress in your life, and knowing how to get yourself back on track. The following questions should help you learn how to make these judgment calls.

1. Make a list of all the different ways stress affects you. Include things like sleep, temper, diet, exercise, studying, etc.

2. Make a list of all the things that help you maintain balance in your life. Include things like exercise, sleep, diet, relationships, fun, etc.

You can also try this "Anti-Worry Technique" for those times when you need to concentrate and study, but are too stressed to hold that concentration for more than a few minutes.

Anti-worrying technique:

1. When you sit down to study, pile a bunch of scrap paper in the upper right-hand corner of your desk.

2. Begin studying. Whenever a worry, concern, or random thought passes through your head, take a piece of paper and write down the worry as concisely as possible. Then put the paper, face down, in a new pile in the upper left-hand corner of your desk. Continue studying.

3. Whenever you notice yourself drifting, repeat Step 2.

4. End your studying time a half hour early.

5. Take the pile that you've written on and browse through them. Pick one that really bothers you and think about it for a while. When you're done, and if you feel like it, pick another.

6. Continue for only one half hour, and then go do something enjoyable.

16

passion, commitment, and success

*I can always be distracted by love, but
eventually I get horny for my creativity.
Gilda Radner*

One of the best things that you can do for yourself (and perhaps one
of the most difficult) is to discover and explore your passion. Once
you're familiar with this part of your life it makes everything easier
and more tolerable. Passion is the most direct route to the most important experience you need to have in high school, and indeed, in
life – the experience of giving 100% to something that's important
to you. To be honest, it almost doesn't even matter what that thing is.
Sharon, 16, finds her passion through dancing:

> When I'm dancing I lose myself, or maybe it's
> that I find myself. I just get lost in the dance,
> in my body moving precisely, in the energy that
> takes me over. It's like a drug for me.
> Sometimes I get scared about certain moves, but
> unlike other places in my life, my fear doesn't
> stop me, it makes me work harder.

Pat, 17, finds his with computers:

I love to go home and work on my computer. I'm really into programming and things like that. I even work part-time at a computer repair shop in town. It just makes me think so hard. There is always another challenge around the corner, and it doesn't matter how difficult it is, I just hang in there until I figure it out.

For Jason, 16, it's basketball:

I would go crazy without basketball. I play all year long. It literally keeps me sane. Whenever things get too crazy for me I just find a hoop and shoot around until I feel better. It always makes me feel better. And because I'm pretty good at it, I work even harder at it. It's great to play on the team with the other guys — we have to count on one another and never give up on one another either. We don't let each other take the easy way out. I know I'm a better person when I'm playing ball than at any other time during the day. It really does keep me sane.

For Jerod, 16, it's art:

I draw or paint almost every day, probably too much. I would much rather paint than do my school work. It's so much more rewarding. When I paint I don't even need anybody to tell me if it's good or not, I know. It's so freeing for me to paint, I just lose track of time and get lost in it. And I always keep challenging myself to do more difficult and creative things in my work. I'm never satisfied, but then again, I'm never _not_ satisfied either.

And Carla, 17, finds passion through music:

I would die without my music. Whenever I have spare time I grab my guitar and play — even if

it's just a few minutes at a time. On weekends
sometimes I'll stay home and play the entire
weekend! I don't go out or even return phone
calls, I just play my music. And it's never the
same. I could play a song 1,000 times and it's
never the same, at least not to me. Sometimes I
play with some other guys in a couple of local
bands, but pretty much I play on my own. When I
go to college I hope to get a band together with
some other students.

There are an endless number of possibilities for what might stir your
passion; your job is to find out what works for you *and to keep yourself involved with it*. Ideally you find this thing in high school, but
there's no guarantee (and indeed, many perfectly well-adjusted people find it much later in life). Whatever your pace, it's important to
set yourself on this track of finding your passion, because when you
have something you really care about in life, everything else is all the
more bearable. Notice how I didn't say "when you have a person to
care for." Ideally, your passion is self-contained (you can do it alone
or with others) and isn't focused on someone else. In other words,
your passion is a self-driven activity or interest.

Discovering your passion

Although everyone can find it, there's no direct path to discovering
your passion. For some people it's a long search, while for others it's
something they just happen upon. Some people have known about it
for as long as they can remember, while still others never do locate it.
Sadly, there's no guarantee that you'll find your passion in life, but
most likely you will. Take a look at the adults around you — what are
each of them passionate about? Maybe you recognize that some seem
to be missing a spark in their lives, but luckily for them, it's never too
late. Everyone's path is different, so start your search now, or, if you
know your passion, make sure you make time for it no matter how
busy you are. As Booker, 17, points out, it can really improve your
outlook:

For most of high school I sort of just went with
the flow. I was okay at most things, but not real

good at anything. But then towards the end of junior year I went on this rock climbing trip with the school. I had never been before. (And the only reason I went this time was because my parents were going out of town, and if I didn't go climbing then I would have had to go with them.) It was amazing! Climbing is so hard and demands so much attention. By the time we finished our first climb I was totally hooked — it was like nothing I had ever experienced before. My friends were astonished — they'd never seen me like this before. I'd never felt like this before! That was the beginning, and now I climb as much as I can — I even joined a climbing wall in the town next to where I live. I drive over at least a couple of times a week to climb on my own and with some of the other climbers I have met there.

Basically, there's no plan to follow for discovering your passion. The closest thing I can offer you is to keep your curiosity and sense of adventure open. If you make a habit of taking risks and trying new things, you might stumble on to something you never even thought of. Says Carolyn, 17:

I had always been kind of curious about the martial arts and all the things those guys could do in the movies. So one day I just signed up for some beginning aikido classes. It was hard at first but by the end of three classes I was really into it. Now [three years later] I am one of the senior students and plan to continue studying it in college next year.

Not everyone's search is as easy as Carolyn's. In fact, if you're serious about discovering your passion, expect a few dead ends along the way. They're part of the searching process, so don't let them knock you down. Ivan, 15, had a good response:

I love to listen to music so I thought it only
made sense that I would love to play it too.
But after trying to learn a couple of different
instruments I realized I'm not into playing
music. I just love to listen.

Commitment

For those of you who have not yet discovered your passion, don't
worry, there's something else equally important – commitment.
Even if you're still searching, making and keeping commitments is
not only possible, but also really important. Your commitments are
things that *you* decide on, that are important to *you* – not what
everybody else tells you is important (even though in some cases they
may be the same). Here's an example of someone who's not sure she
agrees with what her parents and teachers think is important:

I suppose grades are important to me. I mean I
want to get into a good college and everything,
and I have to have good grades for that. At least
my parents and teachers tell me that all the
time. But somehow I just never follow through
on any of these things. When I leave school I
plan to do my homework, but I usually never get
around to it.

Clara's parents and teachers are committed to her getting good
grades, but since she's not committed to them she'll probably always
fall short – until it becomes important to her.

Commitment is something you can cultivate yourself, and it usually arises from either passion or determination (or maybe both).
When you discover your passion, then commitment grows easily
from it, or if you determine that something's important to you, you'll
probably work harder at it. While this second way of developing commitment takes more work, it also gives back lots of satisfaction. Listen to what Phyliss, 16, has to say:

While I'm naturally good at tennis I don't enjoy
it that much. But I decided to give it my best
when I realized that with some work it could

earn me a scholarship to college — and that is the only way I could afford to go. So I made myself practice hard and play often, especially during the summer.

And Sal, 16:

Schoolwork never mattered that much to me, but towards the end of sophomore year I realized that my parents were right — I needed to get better grades to get into college. I never told them they were right though, I just made the decision to do better myself. I couldn't stand the idea of them saying, "We told you so."

The important thing to understand about commitment is that after you decide what's important, you commit yourself to it every day. Things will not happen just because you want them to. In this sense, commitment isn't abstract at all, it's what you do and decide everyday. Shauna, 16, shows the kind of focus it takes:

I committed to being in the play, and even though school is overwhelming right now I still make sure I learn my lines before I do my schoolwork. Right now, doing my best for the play is more important than my schoolwork, but this will change once the play is over.

Shauna raises one critical point, namely that your commitments change over time, depending on where you are as a person. Sometimes you'll make commitments that only last for a specific time – a season, production, semester, or summer – and other commitments will be more indefinite, lasting through high school and even into adulthood.

Success

Once you know what's important to you and have made a commitment to it, you have to figure out how to succeed at it. Knowing what you want and getting it are two very different things, and while almost everyone wants to be successful, not many people know how to do it. Or, one might venture to say, few people are willing to put in the work it takes to become successful. And fewer still understand the kind of work that's necessary to ensure success – most just "want to do better" or think that just working harder is the answer. It really takes focus and a plan. Listen to Adam, 15:

```
I want to be a better student, so next semester
I am going to work much harder. I'll do all my
homework and pay better attention in all my
classes. I'm really going to work hard.
```

Or Jill, 16:

```
I want to improve my tennis game over the summer.
I'm going to play every day and really work at
getting better.
```

Both Adam and Jill have very heartfelt goals, but they'll probably last about as long as most New Year's resolutions. Why? Their vows are simply too vague. Exactly how are they going to improve? In what areas? How will they measure their improvement? What strengths do they have to build on? What weaknesses need improvement? Until they spell out the means to an end, there's not much chance of long-term success. This is precisely what happened to Celeste, 16:

```
At first I did better in my classes, well at
least in a couple of them. But now [six weeks
later] things are pretty much the same as they
were last semester. I'm not sure what happened.
It sort of all faded. Maybe next year.
```

Don't worry though, there are some strategies which will help you clarify your plan of attack. I'm going to focus here on academics because, like it or not, they probably really are the biggest part of high school. Still, the methods presented can work with almost any area of your life that matters to you – feel free to substitute whatever is important to you, like painting, sports, drama, or community service.

Like adults, you wake up five days a week and go to work. The only difference is that your work is solely about learning, and you don't get paid for it, yet. However, the amount you eventually get paid at your job will have a lot to do with the studying and learning you do now in high school. Don't kid yourself either, your education *is* your best investment in the future. And please, don't confuse education with grades – they aren't the same things.

Let's say you commit to being a good student. From this commitment comes the motivation and willingness to address the areas that don't come naturally to you or which you aren't automatically interested in. This is hard work, but it's also extremely rewarding. In fact, understanding and working on the things that don't come easily to you is the cornerstone of any formula for success. Greta, 15, has the right idea:

> Even though math is my worst subject it is what I make myself do first when I start my homework, otherwise I'll never give it my full attention — if any attention at all. It's my hardest subject and the one I do worst in, but I know it makes me a better student. Math forces me to be a more organized and responsible student, even though I don't like it at all.

For most students, this concept of prioritizing your effort and addressing the hardest things first comes naturally in all areas except academics. Lisa, 16, automatically applies it to her basketball:

> I don't dribble [a basketball] well with my left hand, so whenever I practice I make sure to do most of my dribbling with my left hand. It takes a lot more of my attention, but I know that I'm getting better with my left hand and definitely better as a player. Sometimes you have to practice the things you don't like to do in order to get better.

So why should your school work be any different? Put simply, if you want to be a better student, make your worst subjects and worst habits your first priority – you'll always have the time and energy for the areas that come naturally to you. Besides, following this practice now better prepares you for the work world, where every job has something about it that you won't like (sad, but true). Listen to Dylan, 20:

> I like just about every part of my job as restaurant manager except the scheduling of shifts. For the first few months I waited until the last possible minute and then never did a very good job because I didn't give myself enough time. After three months I met with the owner for my first evaluation, and she gave me high marks in everything except scheduling. We talked for a while, and she suggested that because it was the thing I needed to work on the most, I should make it the first thing I do every week. I resisted the idea at first, but she is my boss — and I have learned never to argue with the boss, at least if you like your job — so I went along with the idea. She was right. Now, two months later, scheduling, while not much fun, is also not a big deal.

Goals and organization

Let's start by setting some smaller goals as part of your larger commitment. Goals are the outcomes you want for yourself – better grades, more tackles per game, or a lead role in the play. The next step involves organizing the details of what you're going to do to achieve your goal. There are many theories about how to do this, but generally it all comes down to seven essential points, listed below. Again, for the purposes of consistency, academics are used for this example, but the seven points are applicable anywhere.

1. **General Goal:** What do you want?

2. **Specific Goal:** Spell out the general goal in specific and measurable terms.

3. **Steps:** What steps are involved in achieving the goal?

4. **When:** Determine exactly when you will do these things.

5. **Reality Check:** Is this too ambitious?

6. **Do It:** Get started.

7. **Evaluation:** How well did you do? Where do you go next?

Here's an example of how this would apply to schoolwork:

1. **General Goal:** I want to be a better student.

2. **Specific Goal:** I want a B average, with no grade below a C.

3. **Steps:**
    a. Clean off my desk.
    b. Go to all my classes.
    c. Meet with my math teacher to get caught up.
    d. Do two hours of homework a night.
    e. Do biology first – it's my worst subject.

4. **When:**
    a. Clean off my desk.
        Tonight.
    b. Go to all my classes.
        Starting tomorrow.
    c. Meet with my math teacher to get caught up.
        Next Monday after school.
    d. Do two hours of homework a night.
        Start next Monday.
    e. Do biology first – it's my worst subject
        Tonight.

5. **Reality Check:**
    a. Clean off my desk.
        Tonight. *Can do.*
    b. Go to all my classes.
        Starting tomorrow. *Can do.*
    c. Meet with my math teacher to get caught up.
        Next Monday after school. *Can't do. I have an away game after school on Monday and a home game on Tuesday. I could do it Wednesday, but Thursday is more realistic.* **Change this to next Thursday.**
    d. Do two hours of homework a night.
        Start next Monday. Can't do. *I do about ten minutes a night now. From ten minutes to two hours would be like going from*

running one lap around the track to a marathon! I will add five minutes a night until I get to ninety minutes (two hours is way too ambitious!). This will take 16 nights. **Change to ninety minutes of homework a night beginning three weeks from today.**

    e. Do biology first – it's my worst subject
        Tonight. *Can do.*

6. **Do it.** *Starting now.*

7. **Evaluation:** At the end of the quarter I will see if got a B average with nothing below a C. If so, I'll keep up the same pace; if not, then I'll have to add something, maybe more homework time.

THINK ABOUT IT

Pick an area of your life where you want more success and apply the seven step model we just discusssed. The good news is that, with just a little practice, you'll start to internalize your goal setting and planning, and eventually the process will become a standard part of how you think. Good luck, but then again, luck doesn't have much to do with it.

MORE READING:

Who Cares What I Think: American Teens Talk About Their Lives and Their Country by Marcia A. Thompson.
What Color is Your Parachute? by Richard Nelson Bolles.

#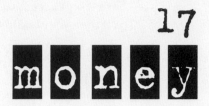

17

> I'd like to live like a poor man with
> lots of money.
>
> Pablo Picasso

Everyone knows all too well what money is and, more or less, how it works. Very few of us, on the other hand, have any understanding of our relationship to money. Most people love having money but hate thinking about it – other than fantasizing about winning the lottery. People have more trouble talking honestly about money than just about anything else, even sex. If you don't believe me, try it. Ask your parents how much money they make, or, ask some of your teachers the same question. Ask a classmate how much money they have in the bank, or where they get their spending money. Most people get really embarrassed by these kinds of questions; many find it embarrassing just to *think* about asking the question. As you approach adulthood, now is as good a time as any to begin to understand your relationship to money, and since it's doubtful that any of your school courses will cover the subject, it's up to you to learn.

One pretty standard concept is that if you're old enough to drive a car, you're certainly old enough to have a working bank account. It doesn't matter if you have $10 or $10,000 to your name, you should still have a savings account, especially since most banks don't charge for savings accounts. If your parents haven't already suggested this to you then you should take the initiative yourself. Here's why:

1. You need to become knowledgeable about money and financial institutions – they are a part of your day-to-day life, and keeping your head in the sand is not a useful option.
2. When you take this kind of initiative your parents have to start seeing you as responsible, as you're showing off your responsible side.
3. It feels good to figure out this aspect of your life, and to be in control of your finances.

One big reason why being in control of your monetary situation helps is because most of you want to drive. This certainly means you'll have to get car insurance. If your parents are up to handling this payment you're in good shape, but you should still understand what it's all about. Ask one of them to go through the insurance policy with you, or enlist someone's help.

If your parents are requiring you to pay your own car insurance, then you have to start thinking early on about where that money's going to come from. Even if you have an allowance, it's unlikely that it goes beyond your day-to-day expenses. Well, start getting used to the idea of a budget. This may involve a summer job or part-time work during the year, either outside the home or a job you negotiate with your parents at home. Both have their ups and downs. Alicia, 16, talks about working at home:

> I tried working for my dad at his office at home, but it was a disaster. Finally I just got this part-time job at the local video store. It's much, much better. I get a check every two weeks and everything at work is real clear — my boss is just my boss. It was too confusing having my father as my boss and my dad.

But for Chay, 17, working at home has been just fine:

> I have been doing a couple of hours of yard work every Saturday since eighth grade [she

is now a junior] and it has worked out great.
If something comes up I just tell my mom and
we agree to another time to get the work done.
I really like the flexibility, plus I like
working on our yard instead of someone else's.
This way I get to enjoy the work I have
done too.

However you get it, the bottom line is the same – money is a means to an end. It buys the things you need and want, but also costs you time and energy to get. Says Sam, 17:

My friends all think it's pretty cool that I
work 20 hours a week. They are real jealous
of the money I have, and the freedom from my
parents it gives me. I like all that too. It's
just that sometimes nobody sees how hard it is
to miss so much hanging around time and study
time. Work takes longer than 20 hours a week —
there is time spent getting ready, coming home,
and coming down from my shift. There is no way
I can go straight from work to doing my homework
or going to sleep. I'm way too wired to get anything like that done.

So part of understanding your relationship with money is deciding what you're willing to give up for it in terms of free time and energy. This involves some prioritization on your part (review the previous chapter for some help defining your goals). Ultimately, the goal is to have making money become a balanced part of your life. Shannon, 16, has the following attitude toward making money:

I like to babysit because I can arrange it
according to my schedule. During soccer season I
only babysit once in awhile because of practice,
games, and keeping up in school. Also, during
exams I hardly ever take a job. But during vacations I really load up. That way I've got some
spending money when school starts up again.

And Katie, 16:

> I work a couple of nights a week as a busperson
> at a restaurant in town. What's cool about the
> job is that a lot of my friends work there too.
> So if one of us needs a night off, all we have
> to do is get someone to cover for us. The boss
> doesn't care, as long as one of us is there. But
> if we mess up, and nobody shows, then he holds
> the person scheduled to work responsible.

Once you figure out how much time you can spare, then you have to find something that will pay you money for your efforts. Obviously, the higher paying the job, the better, but there are other things to consider besides the wage. Do you like what you'll be doing? Are you learning something useful? Is there flexibility? Will it lead to more full-time work in the summer? Is there a future in this kind of work? It's very important to realize that sometimes the best-paying job is not the best job for you. But at other times, good money and good work do go hand in hand, as it did for Michael, 17:

> I took a summer job as a carpenter's helper. It
> was real hard work and I got paid well too. I
> worked full-time all summer. The best part was
> that I learned a lot about carpentry, and who
> knows, maybe I'll be a carpenter one day. The
> worst part was not having much energy at night to
> do anything besides eat. But weekends were great.

Stephanie, 17, made her decision based upon the money she might make in the future:

> I could have had two jobs — working at a video
> store or busing tables in a restaurant. The
> video store paid a little more and seemed like
> easier work, but I picked the restaurant because
> I knew that if I did well they would make me a
> waitress. And as a waitress I would make a lot
> more than either at the video store or busing
> tables.

In terms of landing a job, Jeff Tyler wrote the following article in his school newspaper, *The Marin Academy Voice*, which offers some good tips:

If you want to find some way to get extra cash over the summer but have serious moral conflicts with robbing banks, then you have just one option. You need to get a job. There are two types of jobs you can get. The first type is the job that one of your relatives gives you, running errands to the office or store for eight dollars an hour. That is really just a gift. The other type is the one involving going out into the work place and selling yourself to potential employers. The rest of this article will concentrate on the latter.

If you haven't squared away a job by this point in time [end of May], you're on the late side. That doesn't mean, though, that all hope is lost. From my own experience last summer, there will still be enough opportunities. I didn't even think about getting a job until after school had gotten out. When time is running short, the best thing to do is to look for "help wanted" signs in places like coffee shops and ice cream parlors. Another good way to find a job is to talk to your friends who have had jobs, and learn where they worked, how they heard about the job, and what they did to get it.

When you do find a job opening, go and get the application right away. Complete the form as thoroughly and thoughtfully as possible. When filling out the "previous employment" section, be sure to list any activities that would show that you have had responsibilities, especially community service. Don't forget to include things such as baby-sitting and yard work. Make yourself seem as active and useful as possible.

The key to the inevitable interview is
manners. They count big time. The people hiring
want somebody to treat their customers respect-
fully and politely. Your manners and friendly
personality will show how well you deal with
serving others. Look normal for the interview
(employers are put off by kids who dress funny).
One last, often overlooked, point to a successful interview is to arrive on time at the least,
though a couple of minutes early is better. With
a little luck an employer will offer you a job.
When this happens, adjust your schedule to fit
theirs; be accommodating. It may not come on the
first try, but don't be discouraged, keep trying.
There is a job for you.

THINK ABOUT IT

At some point you're going to need a resume. Resumes are easy-to-
read, one page summaries of your work related experiences, which
give potential employers a snapshot of your work experiences. Every
resume should include your name, address, and telephone number, a
history of education and previous employment, a list of special inter-
ests, and information about your references. Once you have a resume, filling out job applications is a breeze. This exercise helps you
organize your experiences should you ever want to make your own
resume.

1. Make a list of every paying job you've ever had. Make sure to include things like paper routes, yard work, and jobs around your
   home.

2. Make a list of all the volunteer work you've done. Include things like fund-raising car washes, volunteer tutoring, and coaching.

3. List two adults and one friend who know you well and who would speak highly of you in terms of your level of responsibility and maturity.

   a.

   b.

   c.

This is all you need to complete just about any job application. Now you have two choices – you can either use this information to fill out job applications that interest you, or you can use it to design your own one-page resume.

MORE READING:

How To Be A Super Sitter by Dr. Lee Salk and Jay Litvian.

Rules For Writers: A Brief Handbook by Diana Hacker.

The Complete Resume and Job Search Book For College Students by Bob Adams with Laura Morin.

18
the college decision

My idea of education is to unsettle
the minds of the young and inflame
their intellects.
      Robert Maynard Hutchins

As the end of high school approaches you have to decide if college is for you. While college might not be for everyone, it is for more of you than you realize. Don't sell yourself short when making this decision. Listen to what Kevin, 20, did:

> It was during my second semester senior year
> that I finally decided I wanted to go to college.
> It was too late for me to apply to a four-year
> college — besides, I had terrible grades — but
> not too late to get into community college.
> I ended up spending two years at community
> college and then transferring to a four-year
> college. It was definitely the hard way to do it,
> but I did it.

You must understand that going to college doesn't necessarily mean that you have to have terrific grades. Sure, it helps to have a strong

146

academic record, and it definitely gives you more choices, but it's not essential if you're willing to work hard. As the old saying goes, where there's a will there's a way.

Many of you have already made the decision to go to college, like Shane, 18:

```
I guess I had always assumed that I would go to
college. I really have no idea what I want to do
in terms of work so it seems like college is a
good next step.
```

And Bert, 17:

```
I have known since about the sixth grade that
I wanted to be a contractor like my dad. While I
don't have to go to college for this work I still
want to go. It will make me a more well-rounded
person no matter what kind of work I end up
doing. Besides, I want to go for the whole
college experience.
```

Others of you have already decided that college is *not* for you, like Tiffany, 18:

```
There is no way I'm going to college. The class-
room and I just don't get along. I need to get
out there and do something.
```

Whichever way you choose to go, I still recommend that you read the rest of this next section – just in case. If you're undecided, then reading this might help you decide, and by all means, if you're planning to go to college, read on to get familiar with what's required.

Financing colleges falls into the "if there's a will there's a way" category, too. If you're admitted to a college, that college's financial aid office will do everything it can to make it possible for you to attend. While this doesn't necessarily mean a tuition-free four years, it does mean lots of useful and creative information on alternative means of financing your college years: from student loans to ROTC scholarships to all sorts of other things you have yet to imagine. Listen to Sally's story:

I knew that my family couldn't afford college so
I wasn't even planning to apply. But one of my
teachers said I should apply regardless of
money, just to see what would happen. She was
right! I ended up getting a scholarship from a
local school and lots of financial aid. I still
have to take out a loan each year, but it's real
small compared to what it actually costs to go
to college. So next month I'm going to be the
first one in my family to go to college.

Another point to consider is that you don't have to have your career
all planned out and know what you want to study before you actually
go to college. In fact, most freshmen have no clue what they're going
to concentrate on, and indeed most college students change their
major *at least* once during college. Carol, 22, had this experience:

When I went to college I had no idea what I
wanted to study. By the time I graduated I had
tried two different majors — English and Sociol-
ogy — before finally deciding on Business. Most
of my friends changed majors at least once, too.

The college application

When you first look at your college applications, you might be completely overwhelmed, but don't worry, they *are* manageable. The basic application is not that difficult or time-consuming, but there are
areas that can be tricky: writing the personal essay, asking teachers
to write recommendations, and dealing with the emotions that go
with applying.

Writing the personal essay is difficult because there's usually so
little direction. The questions are wide-open: "Tell us about yourself,
in 500 words or less;" "Tell us all about a pivotal moment in your
life, in 500 words or less;" "Tell us about someone important in your
life, in 500 words or less." You get the point — most of you will respond to it like Jesse, 17, did:

The essay is so vague I don't know where to start.
I just wish they would tell me what they want.

What's even worse is that you know somebody's going to be making a judgment about you based upon your essay. Without ever meeting you they will make a decision about you as a person, all from 500 words or less. Sophia, 17, shares everyone's concern:

> Whenever I write something I just imagine this old woman sitting there with a red pen making all sorts of marks on my essay, saying things to herself like: "Oh my, this one will never do." And, "Oh, what a stupid mistake to make on an essay." And, "Hmm, quite an ego on this one!" And, "If I don't get some more coffee I'll never get through this one."

The hardest part of the essay is that you don't know your audience. Therefore, it's important to write for yourself; write the essay that you'd like to read. Next, take it to your counselor or English teacher to get some feedback. This will help you tailor the essay *you* like to the tastes of the typical admissions committee. Maine, 17, heeded this advice:

> After I finished the essay I took it to Ms. Peterson to see what she thought. She really liked it, and then she helped me change a few things that highlighted parts of myself that I was too shy to say myself. Her input helped a lot.

It's likely that many people will ask to read your essay, people like your parents. Depending on the relationship, they could be a good source for feedback. At other times, they're the worst, as they try to take over the essay. You have to decide who can read it, when, and how you'll feel about what they say. Remember, it's your essay. Pauline, 17, says:

> My mom really wanted to read my essay, but it was too personal. I wrote about almost being raped junior year, and she doesn't even know about it. I just had to tell her no, no matter how much she tried to guilt me.

And Ryan, 17:

> I let my mom read my essay because it was about
> her and what a good job I thought she did with
> me. It was all the stuff I had never told her.

Or, as a wise teacher named Joe once said:

> For me, the best real test of a college applica-
> tion essay is to read it aloud to a friend. If
> you can do that without feeling like a dork,
> it's probably excellent.

The next thing to think about is getting teachers to write recommendations – not as easy as it sounds. You're asking them to do extra work on your behalf, and you're asking them to say good things about you. In short, when you ask someone to write a recommendation, you leave yourself vulnerable to their reaction. Says Belinda, 17:

> I was so scared when I asked Mr. Thompson to
> write me a recommendation. Even though he offered
> to write it for me last month I was still really
> nervous asking him. I mean he could always say
> no. And what if he didn't feel like he could say
> good things about me?

Here are some things to keep in mind when asking someone to write a recommendation for you:

1. Give them plenty of time. Don't ask them on Monday for a recommendation that you need on Friday. Try to give them two to four weeks notice, *minimum*. They're probably writing more than one recommendation, and also, the more lead time they have the better the letter usually is.
2. Give them all the forms they'll need, as well as an addressed *and stamped* envelope to send the letter directly to the school in.
3. A few days before the recommendation is due, send them a short thank-you card. This either makes them feel good about the letter they've written or gets them in gear if they've procrastinated!

Finally, the emotions that go with applying to college aren't as easily described as writing the essay and getting recommendations is. Everyone reacts to the application process differently, depending on their personality, family, and academic goals. For some, applying to college is the most stressful event of high school, as it was for Stewart, 17:

```
Applying to college nearly killed me. I put
all sorts of ridiculous pressure on myself. It
felt like if I didn't get into a "name" school
then everyone would think I was a failure —
myself included. And my parents didn't help at
all — they both expected me to get into a good
school and weren't shy about telling me. I hated
it all.
```

For others like Wanda, 17, the application is just another thing to do in high school:

```
I never doubted I was going to go to college, so
during the end of junior year I went on a college
trip with my dad to get a feel for some different
schools. Then that fall I made a list of six
places I liked. My college counselor looked the
list over with me and added two more and
subtracted one — she wanted to make sure there
were at least two schools where my admission was
a pretty sure thing. It was not a big deal. My
parents have always said that my attitude about
college is more important than the actual
college I attend, and I agree.
```

Probably the most important thing to remember is that colleges are all more similar than different, so first decide on which things are important to you, and then use those criteria for picking schools.

After you've picked your schools and completed and mailed in the applications, you start the long, arduous process of waiting. Most applications are due in late December or early January, and since most schools send out admissions letters on April 15, this leaves you with at least four months of waiting. You're probably going to find your-self facing down second semester, senior year with lots of stuff up in the air.

Second semester senior year

This semester is one of the most overrated phenomena known to hu-mankind. It's not the big party or love-in portrayed in the movies. Rather, it goes from being sometimes exhilarating to sometimes lonely, sometimes sad to sometimes content. It's a confusing last se-mester of school. Think about it. On the one hand, you're leaving high school and entering the adult world. You're more in charge of your life than ever before . . . what could be better? But on the other hand, you're leaving a place that you've known well for four years. (And whether you liked high school or not, you were probably com-fortable there.) You're leaving the tight social world of your friends, and you'll probably not see each other like this ever again. And you're getting ready to enter the unknown world of college or work, where you'll have to start all over again to prove yourself and make friends. That's a lot to swallow, as Clint, 18, found out:

> Second semester surprised me. I expected to feel great. But instead I was pretty lonely. Sure, we all partied a lot and smiled and laughed, but underneath it all I was sad to be leaving and scared to be going to college. This is not to say that I wanted to stay in high school either — just that graduating was harder than I thought it would be.

Or Max, 17:

> I'm ready to go to college, I'm just not ready to leave high school.

One of the best things you can do for yourself during this time is to check in with the people who have mattered the most during the past four years. Let them know that they mattered, as Susan, 18, did:

> I took my English teacher out for lunch right after graduation to thank her for supporting me

through all my ups and downs. It was nothing
fancy, but it felt good to do it.

And Eric, 17:

I made sure to let my three closest friends
know how much they meant to me these last four
years. It was nothing too mushy; I just needed
to acknowledge them.

Similar gestures are equally well appreciated by your family, especially if you're going away to college. Believe it or not, parents often feel abandoned by their kids when they go off to college, so make sure to spend some time touching base with them and with your brothers and sisters, too, if you have them. Says Chauncy, 18:

A week or so after I graduated my parents took
all of us away for the weekend. At first I didn't
want to go, but I could see it was important to
them. We just hung out together at a lake all day
Saturday. But after dinner that night they gave
me a photo album of my high school years. It was
really cool. We stayed up real late talking
about all the different things that had happened
in just four years.

Graduating from high school and moving on to your next phase of life is a big deal for everybody. Like the beginning of high school was, it's confusing, exciting, somewhat unpredictable, and usually, better than you expected. Enjoy your last semester knowing that you will hold onto the friends that are truly important to you and that you'll make new friends as you move forward. Also, never forget that your family will always be there for you, and remember to have fun.

THINK ABOUT IT

Before you apply to college, you need to decide on what kind of place you want to spend the next four years in. This should help.

1. Clarify what you're looking for in a collage by addressing each of the topics below:

a. Size of school:

b. Geographic location and climate:

c. Course offerings:

d. Distance from home:

e. Activities outside of the class:

f. Cost:

g. Diversity:

h. Reputation:

i. Other qualities you're looking for:

2. Now go back and prioritize these criteria – make yourself rank your preferences. This will help narrow the field considerably.

3. Now look at your potential schools – which best fits your list?

MORE READING:

Athletic Scholarships: A Complete Guide by Conway Greene.

The Scholarship Book: A Complete Guide to Private-Sector Scholarships, Grants and Loans for Undergraduates by Daniel J. Cassidy.

10 Minute Guide To Getting Into College by O'Neal Turner.

100 Successful College Application Essays by Chrisotpher J. Georges and Gigi Georges (Editors).

wrap up

High school is going to be different for everybody, yet the basic struggles are surprisingly similar. I hope that in some small way, this book has helped you understand yourself a little bit better. More to the point, I hope it has helped you become more compassionate with yourself and with those around you. As a wise friend of mine once advised, don't try to be perfect, it's overrated. Try instead to be good, because if you're good then you'll learn equally well from both your joy *and* pain. This will lead you to be fully human, and when all is said and done, that's the best any of us can hope for. Good luck, and keep an eye out for one another now, and as you get older too.

acknowledgments

Again, I offer my most profound thanks to Megan Twadell-Riera and Joe DiPrisco. Without your faith, and very real assistance, this project would have forever remained a "good idea." Thanks again. Also, special thanks to Karen Blanpied for compassionately reading an early draft — we must be good friends for me to have let you read such a rough piece of work! Thanks.

Special thanks to the team of people that pulled this book together in its final form. First to all the folks at Celestial Arts. There is no way one person can make something like this happen. Thanks to David Hinds, publisher, Christa Laib, editor, Fuzzy Randall, managing editor, and Leili Eghbal, Cynthia Traina, and Cindy Cohen of the publicity department.

Also, thanks to my agent Peter Beren, without whom I might still be peddling my ideas on the street. And, of course, thanks to my publicist Khris Lundy, without whose work this book might quietly rest on a library shelf somewhere instead of in your hands.

Finally, a huge thanks to all the students and families who have entrusted me with their stories. (In this regard, a special thanks to Annie Schowalter.) Truly, without all of you, this book would not have been possible.